Welcome back to Penhally Bay!

Mills & Boon® Medical™ Romance welcomes you back to the picturesque town of Penhally, nestled on the rugged Cornish coast! With sandy beaches and breathtaking landscapes Penhally is a warm, bustling community, cared for by the Penhally Bay Surgery team, led by the distinguished and commanding Dr Nick Tremayne.

We're bringing you four new books set in this idyllic coastal town, where fishing boats bob up and down in the bay, friendly faces line the cobbled streets, and romance flutters on the Cornish sea breeze! We've got gorgeous Mediterranean heroes, top-notch city surgeons, and the return of Penhally's very own bad-boy rebel! But that's not all…

We step back into the life of enigmatic, guarded hero Dr Nick Tremayne, and nurse Kate Althorpe—the one woman who has stolen Nick's heart and the only woman he won't allow himself to love! Dr Nick's unquestionable professional skill and dedication to the Penhally Bay Surgery hide his private pain— his is a story that will pierce your heart.

So come in and meet them for yourself…

Dear Reader

You could have knocked me down with the proverbial feather when my editor asked me to write a book as part of the *Brides of Penhally Bay* series. I was almost as excited as when she told me Mills and Boon were going to publish my first book! But I was nervous too. Especially when I found out that the other writers were much-loved authors who had already written books for the first series.

I needn't have worried. The other authors took me under their wing and gave me loads of support and help—and for that I am indebted to them. It was also great fun. We chatted by e-mail almost daily, discussing plot lines and characters until Penhally Bay became almost as well-known to me as my own family. I'm going to miss it!

I do hope you enjoy the story I have written. Annie is an ordinary girl who has something extraordinary happen to her after she meets gorgeous obstetrician Raphael Castillo while in Spain mourning the loss of her future. Happy reading!

Anne Fraser

SPANISH DOCTOR, PREGNANT MIDWIFE

BY
ANNE FRASER

 MILLS & BOON

To Audrey. Thanks for your wonderful company in Spain.

All the characters in this book have no existence outside
the imagination of the author, and have no relation
whatsoever to anyone bearing the same name or names.
They are not even distantly inspired by any individual
known or unknown to the author, and all the incidents
are pure invention.

First published in Great Britain 2009
Large Print edition 2010
Harlequin Mills & Boon Limited,
Eton House, 18-24 Paradise Road,
Richmond, Surrey TW9 1SR

© Harlequin Books S.A. 2009

Special thanks and acknowledgement are given
to Anne Fraser for her contribution to the
Brides of Penhally Bay series

ISBN: 978 0 263 21087 3

Printed and bound in Great Britain
by CPI Antony Rowe, Chippenham, Wiltshire

Anne Fraser was born in Scotland, but brought up in South Africa. After she left school she returned to the birthplace of her parents, the remote Western Islands of Scotland. She left there to train as a nurse, before going on to university to study English Literature. After the birth of her first child she and her doctor husband travelled the world, working in rural Africa, Australia and Northern Canada. Anne still works in the health sector. To relax, she enjoys spending time with her family, reading, walking and travelling.

Recent titles by the same author:

THE PLAYBOY DOCTOR'S SURPRISE
   PROPOSAL
FALLING FOR HER MEDITERRANEAN BOSS
POSH DOC CLAIMS HIS BRIDE
HER VERY SPECIAL BOSS

BRIDES OF PENHALLY BAY

*Bachelor doctors become husbands and fathers—
in a place where hearts are made whole.*

**Look out for these four books
set in the picturesque town of Penhally,
nestled on the rugged Cornish coast.**

**Last month we were back in Penhally
as bad-boy doc Sam Cavendish
tried to win back his long-lost wife...**
The Rebel of Penhally Bay by Caroline Anderson

**This month midwife Annie
meets gorgeous Spanish doctor
Dr Raphael Castillo, and one magical night
leads to one little miracle...**
Spanish Doctor, Pregnant Midwife
by Anne Fraser

**Next month there's a real treat in store as
gorgeous high-flying heart surgeon James
arrives in Penhally!**
Falling for the Playboy Millionaire
by Kate Hardy

**And then there's a new GP in town when
Italian doctor and single father Luca d'Azzaro
brings his twin babies to Penhally**
A Mother for the Italian's Twins
by Margaret McDonagh

**Available from
Mills & Boon® Medical™ Romance**

CHAPTER ONE

ANNIE slid into a pew of the cool, cavernous Spanish church and let the peace wash over her bruised and battered soul.

In two days' time, her holiday would be over and she would be returning to England and Penhally Bay. Which meant work and reality.

Despite her parents' entreaties that she join them on at least part of their Christmas and New Year worldwide cruise, Annie had insisted that she wanted to take this break on her own. Once and for all, she had told them gently, she needed to put her heartache behind her, including the break-up with her fiancé Robert and especially the horribly cruel reason behind it. The last thing she needed was to be on a luxury liner filled with happy families or, even worse, spend Christmas in Scotland with her sister Fiona and her young family. Even staying in Penhally Bay for the holiday season would be more than she could bear.

But her holiday to the small whitewashed village in Andalucia *had* helped. She had spent the days tramping the narrow streets and walking the hills, tiring herself out until she had fallen into bed too exhausted even to dream. Although nothing would ever take away the terrible void in her life, she was beginning to feel she could face the future. Whatever it might bring.

A group of excited children accompanied by a heavily pregnant woman disturbed the silence. As Annie looked at the brown-faced children with their heads of shiny dark hair, she felt her heart tighten. One little girl in particular caught her attention. Unlike the others, she was subdued, her thumb stuck in her mouth as she looked about her with wide-eyed solemnity. She hung back from the rest of the group, resisting the pregnant woman's attempts to pull her into the circle.

Annie followed the youngsters with her eyes, wondering once more what it would have been like if she had been able to have children of her own. She eyed the expectant mother's bump enviously. She must be nearly at term and Annie would have given anything to be in her position.

She would even have been prepared to adopt. God knew, there were enough children out there who needed the pent-up love Annie had to give and she knew she would have made a good mum, if only she had been given the chance. She sighed. But men didn't seem to think that way. Was it so very different for them? After she had accepted that she'd never be able to conceive naturally, she had suggested to Robert that they consider adoption. But he had been horrified at the idea, and over the following months he had withdrawn from her bit by bit until she had finally forced the truth out of him. He couldn't face a future without children. His *own* children. It had been a double blow to her when he had left. She had thought he had loved her. Well, no more. From now on it was just her, by herself. And she would manage. More than manage, she told herself firmly. She would throw herself into her work at Penhally Bay. She would make a good life on her own. It was the start of a new year and a new beginning. Of that she was determined.

Squaring her shoulders, Annie slung her bag over her shoulder and stood up. She had only taken a few steps when she heard a cry of pain ringing out and she swung round to see the heavily pregnant woman bent over, clutching at her stomach.

Instantly, Annie was by her side.

'What is it?' she asked. 'Are you okay?'

The woman stared at Annie with enormous brown eyes stretched with pain and fear.

'*Bebé,*' she gasped. And then doubled over again.

'When is your baby due?' Annie asked, keeping her voice calm, but the woman just frowned at her and shook her head. It was obvious she spoke no English. Annie bit back a sigh of frustration. Although she had learned a few words of Spanish, it wasn't up to the demands of the occasion. She needed someone to translate. And soon.

'She say the baby is coming. Now.'

Annie placed a hand on the woman's abdomen and felt the contractions. She counted slowly. They were coming one after the other, at two-minute intervals. She was absolutely right. The baby was on its way.

Annie lowered herself to the level of the little girl. 'What's your name, sweetheart?'

'Maria.' She gestured to the woman. 'This is my cousin, Señora Lopez.' She removed her thumb for only as long as it took to impart the information.

'Okay, Maria, I need you to be my helper. Can you do that?' When the little girl nodded her head, Annie continued, raising her voice above the babble of excited voices.

'Has your cousin other children?'

Maria nodded again. 'Three.'

'Ask her if they were normal deliveries. Then find out if anyone has a phone. We need to call an ambulance.'

An older woman with a nut-brown face pulled a mobile out of the pocket of her cavernous overall and, muttering something frustratingly incomprehensible to Annie, punched numbers into the phone. Hopefully she was calling an ambulance.

In the meantime, Maria had spoken to the labouring woman and listened to her reply.

'She say her other children all come quickly. This baby not supposed to be here for another few weeks.'

'Okay Maria, Well done. I need to find somewhere private for Mrs Lopez to lie down. Could you ask if there is such a place?'

As Maria spoke to the watching, chattering audience, Annie felt her hand being squeezed tightly as another contraction racked Señora Lopez's body. It was clear that the baby was going to be born right here. Annie guessed it would take time they didn't have for the ambulance to get here from the nearest town. The narrow, winding roads weren't built for speed.

Suddenly the crowd of chattering women parted and a dark-haired man pushed his way through. Annie only had time to note deep brown eyes and high cheekbones. The man spoke in rapid Spanish to the distraught woman holding Annie's hand and Annie saw her visibly relax.

'*Mi hijo,*' the older woman with the mobile said, nodding down at him. '*Médico.*'

My son. Doctor. Annie felt a wash of relief. At least she wasn't on her own any more. She prayed he could speak English. It would take the responsibility of translating from Maria. Although the little girl was doing her best, waiting for her questions and commands to be translated was frustratingly slow.

The man bent over and scooped the woman into his arms as if she weighed nothing. His mother gestured him to follow her while the other women took control of the children. Annie noticed that little Maria followed behind, obviously feeling as if she had a stake in the drama.

'I'm a midwife,' Annie said as she followed the dark-haired man with his burden to the rear of the church. 'Do you speak English?'

For a second, he stopped and looked at Annie. His mouth quirked. '*Sí.* Yes, I speak English. I am Dr Raphael Castillo, obstetrician. My mother has called an ambulance, but it will be some time before it gets here. It has to come from the city and the roads aren't very good. Have you made an assessment?'

'I haven't had a chance to examine her properly, but the contractions are coming one after the other. She could deliver at any time.'

He nodded. 'I think you are correct.' He smiled, flashing even white teeth. 'Looks like it is going to be you and me delivering this baby— right here.'

As he spoke, Señora Lopez cried out again, followed by a string of Spanish words. Dr Castillo responded in the same language as he laid her down on a couch in the priest's room.

'She says the baby is coming,' he said, stripping off the jacket of his suit and rolling up the sleeves of his white shirt. 'There is no more time.'

Noticing a sink at one end of the room, Annie crossed to it and began to scrub her hands. Dr Castillo, speaking to Señora Lopez over his shoulder, joined her. It was obvious from the look on Señora Lopez's face that she knew that the baby was going to be delivered in this tiny room. At least it wasn't a stable, Annie thought wryly. Then while the dark-haired doctor finished rinsing the soap from his hands, Annie examined the woman.

'The head is crowning, Dr Castillo,' she called over. 'I'll deliver the baby if you tell her what to do.' She turned to Maria, who had slipped in beside them. 'Go and see if you can find some towels, sheets anything. Something to wrap the baby in.'

As Maria ran off, Annie turned to him. 'How many weeks is she?'

'Thirty-nine,' he said. Although heavily accented, his English was perfect.

'How sure of her dates is she?'

'She is certain. By the way, her name is Sophia.' Then he turned back and said something to Sophia. Annie didn't need to understand the words to know that he would be telling her to push.

Just as Maria and the doctor's mother appeared at the door with a bundle of shawls and scarves, the baby's shoulder appeared. But then, to Annie's horror, the baby's progress down the birth canal halted. It was stuck. She felt her own heart rate rise. Where was that ambulance? But in the same moment Annie realised that even if it turned up in the next few minutes, it wouldn't help. Sophia was in no position to be moved right now.

She looked up and found Raphael Castillo's calm brown eyes on hers.

'What is it?' he asked quietly.

'The baby's stuck,' she said. 'I think we have a shoulder dystocia.' Seeing the answering look of concern in Raphael's eyes, Annie knew he grasped the gravity of the situation. If they were in a hospital, it would be serious enough, but here, without instruments, not even a pair of forceps, there was every chance they could lose the baby. She stood aside to let him examine Sophia while Maria and the older woman watched silently from the doorway. Sensing something was wrong, the labouring woman called out in panic. Raphael's mother rushed to her side and spoke softly to her. What ever she said seemed to reassure the woman and she flopped back down.

After another couple of minutes of Sophia pushing and the baby not making any progress, Annie was certain they were in serious trouble. It seemed as if Raphael had arrived at the same conclusion.

'I'm going to ask my mother to help me pull Sophia's legs above her shoulders. Then I want you to press down just above the pubic bone as hard as you can.' His expression was grim, but his voice was calm. Somehow Annie felt confident that if anyone could save mother and child, he could.

As soon as Sophia's legs had been manoeuvred into position, Annie followed his instructions. With a cry of pain, Sophia gave a final push and the baby slithered into the Annie's arms, giving a gusty cry a few seconds later. Annie and Raphael's eyes locked over the exhausted mother. He grinned widely, his eyes crinkling at the corners, and Annie's world tilted.

'A healthy baby girl,' he said, repeating the words in Spanish to the new mother.

Quickly Annie checked that the baby's breathing was unrestricted before wrapping the tiny infant in a shawl and passing Sophia her daughter to hold.

'*Gracias, gracias,* Raphael,' Sophia whispered, nuzzling her newborn. She looked up at Annie. '*Gracias, Señora.*' In the distance Annie could hear the sound of a siren approaching. They just had time to deliver the placenta before the ambulance crew hurried in.

Raphael spoke to the paramedics as they prepared to transfer Sophia to the hospital, and Annie studied him surreptitiously. He really was the most gorgeous-looking man she had ever seen in her life! His black wavy hair was worn slightly too long and a lock fell across his eyes. He swept it away impatiently with long, tapered fingers. He had high cheekbones, an aquiline nose and his olive complexion showed off even white teeth. He wasn't overly tall, but every muscle was clearly defined under his white shirt. Tailored trousers clung to thighs that looked as if they had been honed by hours in the gym. All in all he exuded sex appeal. Annie had never met anyone like him before. Quite simply, he took her breath away.

'Well done,' he said to Annie over the cries of the infant. 'I am sorry, I don't even know your name.'

'It's Annie,' she said. 'Annie Thomas. And there's no need to thank me. I was glad to help. Although I'm relieved you appeared when you did. I'm not sure I would have coped—even with my two helpers here.' She nodded at the older woman and the young girl, who were now fussing over the baby.

'My mother—' he indicated the older woman with a nod of his head '—called me. Fortunately, I was waiting for her in a café nearby. She wanted to say a prayer before we went home for lunch.'

His mother glanced up from Sophia and the baby and Raphael introduced them. Señora

Castillo nodded vigorously and said something to her son in rapid Spanish.

'She says you must come for lunch too.' By this time Sophia and her baby were being loaded onto a stretcher, with Raphael helping.

'Shouldn't we go with them to the hospital?' Annie asked.

He looked at her and grinned. 'I will go with them. There is no room for you. Anyway, you are on holiday, no? I am sure you have other things you would like to do. Even if you don't care to join my family for lunch.'

Annie felt unreasonably disappointed. But whether it was because she wouldn't be able to follow up her patient as she was used to doing, or whether it was because Raphael was about to disappear from her life for good, she didn't know. Not that she was in any mood for romance. Not when she had just decided to get her life back on track. The last thing she needed was more complications in her life.

'What about this little one?' Annie asked, indicating Maria, who remained watching with enormous brown eyes.

Raphael laughed and chucked the little girl

under her chin. 'Maria is staying with my mother. She will go home with her. Everyone will be there. It is our New Year family gathering. Maybe you will think about coming and I will see you there later?' He quirked an eyebrow in enquiry and Annie felt a shiver dance down her spine. How on earth was this man having this effect on her? She had only just met him, for goodness' sake! Maybe it was something to do with those intense brown eyes and that body, an inner voice whispered. Maybe it's because she'd never met anyone who looked like him before. Everything about him sent warning signals flashing in Annie's head and she knew the wisest thing she could do was put as much distance as possible between her and this man— and the sooner the better.

As she opened her mouth to protest that she couldn't possibly intrude, Raphael smiled again. 'Actually, you can't say no. Mama will not let you, so you might as well give in now. My mother is—how do you say? Formidable. But, look, I must go. The ambulance is about to leave.' He stared down at her for a long second, holding her gaze with the intensity of his own.

'I hope you will decide to come.' And then he was walking away, leaving Annie reeling.

Sure enough, Mama Castillo was tugging at Annie's arm, making it clear that she expected her to follow. Silently Maria slipped her hand into Annie's and it seemed that she was going for lunch whether she wanted to or not. Well, it wasn't as if she had anything else planned for the rest of the day, and, if she was honest with herself, she'd had enough of her own company. Moreover, hadn't it been one of her New Year resolutions to try and experience more of life? She refused to let herself think too long about the real reason she wanted to go. The thought of seeing Raphael again was irresistible, no matter what the sensible part of her brain was telling her. What could it hurt? She was leaving soon and she would never see any of them again. And what was the point of being wise anyway? Right now, she had nothing left to lose.

'Okay. I'd love to,' she said, finally throwing her hands up in surrender. When Maria translated for her an enormous grin lit up the tiny woman's weatherbeaten face.

They stepped outside just as the ambulance

sped away. Although it was winter, the sun was high in the sky and Annie could feel it warming her skin. She felt a shiver of anticipation. This holiday was turning out to be not at all what she had expected!

Unsure of where they were going or how they were going to get there, Annie was dismayed when Mama Castillo lifted her voluminous skirts and climbed onto a small moped, indicating that Annie should jump on behind her.

Annie looked to Maria for confirmation.

'She says she will take you. I will walk. It is not far. Just up there.' Maria pointed up a narrow road towards a cluster of whitewashed houses. 'In the hills,' she added.

'Could I not walk with you?' Annie said doubtfully. But Maria shook her head decisively. 'No, you must go with Grandma. She says it is too far for an English woman to walk in this sun. I am used to it. It is better if you go on the bike.'

It seemed to Annie as if she had little choice in the matter. Mama Castillo looked in no mood to debate the matter. Reluctantly Annie climbed on the moped and hoped for the best.

In the event Annie kept her eyes closed as they raced up the hill, scattering chickens and goats in all directions. For the whole of the ten-minute journey, Mama Castillo didn't slow down once, not even for a group of men trudging up the hill in front of them. It was obvious to Annie that she only had one speed, and nothing and no one was going to slow her down.

When they eventually stopped outside a farm-house perched on the side of the hill, Annie felt a huge wave of relief. There had been moments when she'd been sure that she wasn't going to survive the journey.

As soon as they climbed off the moped they were surrounded by what seemed to Annie to be most of the village. There were a number of young men, at least two of whom bore a striking resemblance to Raphael, as well as half a dozen women. There were also children, almost too many to count, running around the large court-yard, squealing and laughing.

Overwhelmed by the noise, Annie stood back, feeling suddenly shy. Why on earth had she agreed to come here? she wondered. After a few minutes a stunning woman with thick wavy hair and hazel eyes detached herself from the crowd and came across to Annie holding out her hand.

'Welcome to our home,' she said. 'Mama told me you helped Sophia and her baby today. Sophia is a cousin of my father's so we all are in your debt.' So this dark-haired beauty must be Raphael's sister. Annie could see the resemblance in the high cheekbones and sensuous mouth.

'It was nothing,' Annie replied. 'I was glad to help.'

'My name is Catalina.' The woman continued. 'I heard Raphael was there too.' She stood on tiptoe, looking over Annie's shoulder. 'So where is my brother now? He promised to be here.'

'He went with Sophia and the baby to the hospital. To make sure there were no complications. He said he would come as soon as he was finished there.'

Catalina pouted. 'That's Raphael for you, always working. We don't see him very often. He is supposed to be on holiday with us, just for these few days, but we've hardly seen him. Pah! But seeing as it is our cousin he is attending to, I won't tell him off when he comes.'

And then, before Annie had a chance to say

anything, she was being led into an enormous farmhouse kitchen where a large table had been laid out as if to feed the five thousand. It was covered with bowls of fruit and olives and large platters of paella as well as other Spanish dishes that Annie couldn't identify, but which smelled delicious. Soon she was part of the chattering group, absorbed into their friendly warmth that needed little translation. Catalina made some introductions, but there were too many for Annie to possibly remember all their names. It seemed that she had guessed right and the two men she had thought were Raphael's brothers turned out to be just that. Apart from Catalina, there were another two women who were his sisters. Annie had just been guided into a seat at the table when Maria, smiling shyly appeared silently at her side where, after squeezing in beside her, she remained for the rest of the meal. Gazing around the crowded table, Annie couldn't be sure who Maria belonged to. As far as she could tell, all the children appeared to be shared.

During a spell when no one's attention was on her, Annie wondered wistfully what it would be like to be part of a family just like this one, and in an instant the sadness came flooding back. She squeezed her eyes closed, forcing back the never-far-away tears. She would never know.

When she opened her eyes again, it was to find Raphael looking down at her, his dark-winged brows knotted in puzzlement. His eyes had an intensity that made her feel as if he could see into her soul, and as he held her gaze Annie thought she recognised an answering sadness in their depths, but knew she had to be mistaken. What could this vibrant, gorgeous man have to feel unhappy about? As far as Annie could see, he had everything. Her eyes swept the happy chattering family again; at least, everything that mattered.

He leaned over her. 'Don't be so sad,' he murmured in her ear.

She could smell his aftershave and his breath on her cheek was like a caress. Her heart gave an involuntary leap. What *was* it about him that made her feel like a schoolgirl with her first crush? She couldn't remember the last time she'd had such an instant and powerful response to a man. In fact, she couldn't remember responding like this to a man ever—and that included Robert. Maybe it was the

Spanish sunshine and the couple of glasses of sangria that had been served with lunch. Whatever it was, she couldn't deny she was pleased that he was back before she had made her excuses and left.

'I'm not sad,' she retorted. There was a sudden lull in the conversation and her words rang out around the table. To her acute embarrassment, all eyes swivelled her way. There was a moment of deathly silence before everyone resumed their conversations. Annie felt herself blush to the tips of her ears.

'How is Sophia?' she asked, determined to change the subject.

'Mother and baby are doing fine,' he said. 'She told me to thank you again.' Then he turned towards the others and said something in Spanish to which they all raised their glasses. 'To Sophia! To Annie!' If it were possible, Annie felt more self-conscious than ever, and it seemed by the broad grin on his face that Raphael was enjoying her discomfort.

All of a sudden she wanted nothing more than to put as much distance between herself and this man as possible. She stood, almost knocking over her wineglass in her haste to get away. 'Thank you for the meal, but I really think I should be going,' she said breathlessly. 'I've taken enough of your family's kind hospitality.' She stumbled as her head spun with the sudden movement.

His hand shot out and grasped her wrist, steadying her. The touch of his fingertips seemed to burn her skin.

'I will take you. Where are you staying?'

'Oh, no, it's quite all right. I'm sure I can find my own way. My apartment is opposite the church. It won't take me more than half an hour to walk back. And after that meal, I could do with the exercise.' She was miserably aware that she was babbling on, but she seemed powerless to halt the words erupting from her mouth. The longer she was in his company, the more she felt like a star-struck schoolgirl.

'Anyway, you haven't had a chance to eat yet.' She checked her watch. 'It's almost 5.30! You must be starving by now. Please don't worry about taking me.'

'It is no trouble. My mother would never forgive me my poor manners if I didn't see you home. I told you how formidable she can be. I wouldn't put it past her to—how do you say?—box my ears!'

Annie laughed, suddenly relaxing. 'Okay, then. I wouldn't want to be responsible for that,' she said. 'But I insist you have something to eat before we leave.'

'Only if you promise me you will stay a little longer.' Then he frowned. 'But forgive me, I am stupid. You are sure to have someone waiting for you? Back at your apartment?'

'No,' Annie said heavily. 'I'm on my own, so there isn't really a need for me to rush away.' If she were honest with herself, the last thing she felt like doing was returning to the little flat she had rented. After two weeks of her own company, she was heartily sick of it. Besides, there was something about this family group that made her feel warm and wanted. Perhaps just for tonight she could pretend she belonged and forget about her life back home?

Raphael looked puzzled. 'You are here in Spain on your own? Over Christmas? And New Year! How can that be?'

Annie had no intention of telling him the truth. The last thing she wanted was his sympathy. 'I thought a little bit of winter sun would be nice,' she said.

If anything, Raphael looked even more perplexed. 'It is winter here, too,' he said.

"At home, right now it's snowing.' Annie had to laugh. 'I can assure you there is no comparison.'

'Whatever,' he said, grinning back at her. 'I for one am glad you came to Spain.' There was something in the force of his gaze that sent shivers of anticipation up Annie's spine. 'And I know Sophia is, too,' he added.

The last comment was a reality check. Of course, Annie thought. Why would a man like Raphael Castillo be interested in someone as ordinary as her?

It was growing dark by the time they left and Annie felt a pang as she was subjected to dozens of warm embraces and repeated pleas to return and see them again. All in all, it had been a magical afternoon, and she wished she could stay for ever. But, of course, that wasn't possible. She had her own life to return to even if it was a lonely and barren one—in more ways than one. Just as Raphael opened the wrought-iron gate to the road, Maria came running over and flung herself into Annie's arms, burying her face in Annie's shoulder. Annie felt her heart contract as she cuddled the little girl, breathing in the scent of oranges on her skin. What she would give to be able to hold her own child in her arms.

She released the little girl as Mama Castillo called to her with softly spoken words and Annie watched Maria cuddle up, the inevitable thumb back in her mouth, in the older woman's lap. Regretfully Annie gave a final wave, before following Raphael down the dirt road away from the house.

'Who does Maria belong to?' she asked. 'She is such a sweetheart, but she seems so…I don't know…lost.'

'Ah, little Maria,' Raphael said slowly. 'Her mother, my cousin, died suddenly a few months ago. Her father…' he sucked in his breath, his mouth tightening with disapproval. 'He is weak. He left Maria behind. What kind of man is that? If Maria were my child, I would do everything I could to keep her with me.'

Suddenly the warmth drained from his eyes and Annie shivered. Instinctively she knew that

Raphael was not the kind of man to give up anything he thought he had a right to. He was not the kind of man she would ever want to cross swords with.

'He must have been in some state to abandon his child. People do all sorts of things that are out of character when they are hurting,' Annie said. But she couldn't really understand how any father could abandon his child—especially when that child had just lost her mother. It was too cruel.

'There is no excuse,' Raphael said curtly. 'A father has his duty. How he feels is of no importance when it comes to the child.' He looked away, but not before Annie read the bleakness in his eyes. 'So now she lives with my family. She loves my mother but she still grieves for her own,' Raphael went on. 'She is sad—like you—but every day she is getting stronger.'

There it was again. The reference to her sadness. Was she so transparent? Or did this man just seem to be able to see into her soul?

They walked along the narrow road, the scent of the heavily laden orange trees that edged the pavement drifting in the still air, the velvet sky punctuated with stars. He asked her about her job, and she told him about Penhally Bay, how much she loved living there and how much she enjoyed her job at the hospital. He listened closely, then he told her about his job in Barcelona. That he missed the countryside and regretted that he wasn't able to see his family more often. He grinned down at her.

'As you can tell, we Spaniards are big on family. What about you?'

'I have my parents and a brother as well as a sister. They both have small children. My brother lives in Australia and my parents are going to stay with him there for a few months after their cruise. My sister is in Scotland with her family.' She slid a glance at him. 'I envy you, having your family all so close,' she admitted.

Once again, she thought she saw a shadow pass across his face. But when he smiled she knew she must have been mistaken.

'It's not all good. I have to put up with my sisters and my mother wanting to know everything about my life. *Dios*, they never give me peace.'

Before Annie knew it, they were outside her apartment. The nearby houses were draped in Christmas lights, lighting the cobbled street.

She didn't want the evening to end and it seemed as if Raphael didn't either. He hesitated then said, 'If you are not too tired, there is this little restaurant a few minutes' walk away. It has the most excellent tapas. And I am suddenly hungry again. Will you come with me?'

She let her gaze sweep his muscular frame. There wasn't an ounce of fat on it as far as she could see. Where did he put all that food?

'Okay,' she said softly. 'It's my last night. I might as well make the most of it.'

He steered her towards a small restaurant behind the church. It was packed inside, but there was no one sitting at the outside tables in the plaza.

'Do you mind if we sit here?' Annie asked.

'Of course. If that is what you want.' He took off the thin sweater he had been wearing, revealing a short-sleeved shirt. 'But I insist you put this on.'

Sensing that it would be useless to argue, Annie slipped the sweater on over her shoulders. It smelled faintly of a mix of citrus aftershave and the warm tang of his scent. It was much too large, falling almost to her knees and slipping off her shoulder. Her breath caught in her throat as he leant forward and turned up the cuffs. The gesture was both tender and erotic and as his fingers lightly brushed against her bare skin, Annie felt darts of electricity tingle up her arms.

Raphael studied her slowly, his smile turning up the corners of his mouth and creasing the corner of his eyes. Annie thought yet again that she had never seen a man so gorgeous yet so sure of his masculinity. A part of her, sensing danger, wanted to run from him as fast as she could, but at the same time she knew that she couldn't bear to see him walk out of her life. At least, not yet.

When their order of seafood arrived, it felt like the most natural thing in the world for Raphael to feed her small morsels of lobster and shrimp with his fingers. The touch of his hands on her lips sent small explosions of desire racing through her body.

Then, without saying anything, they stood and Raphael took her hand again. She led him back up the path to the front door of her apartment. Knowing that what was about to happen was beyond her control, she opened the door and, keeping her hand in his, went inside.

'Are you sure?' he said. He looked into her eyes

and it was as if he knew her most hidden thoughts. Despite the ready smile, she saw something in the depths of his ebony eyes that mirrored her own pain. All she wanted was to give comfort and to be comforted in return. The rest of her life could take care of itself.

'It's not too late to change your mind.' His voice was soft, yet there was an undercurrent that caused her pulse to leap.

'No,' she said, stunned by her brazenness. 'It's what I want.' She knew she was risking danger. Not that she didn't trust him—she instinctively knew he would never harm her. But she could no more resist her need for him than she could walk back to Penhally Bay.

He picked up her hand and pressed it to his lips. She shivered as shock waves of desire coursed through her body. She had never experienced lust like it before, but she wasn't naive. She knew what those dark brown eyes were asking her. She didn't want to play games. All she felt was an overriding need to be held in his arms—to have her femininity reaffirmed. It had taken such a beating in the last few months. Surely just this once she could throw caution to the wind and take a chance?

He dropped her hand and pulled her hard against him, one hand on her hip, the other cupping her bottom. She could feel every muscle of his hard chest through his T-shirt and the pressure of his thighs on hers. Flames of desire flooded her body and she turned her face up to his, seeking his mouth. He brought it down on hers, gently at first and then harder as he seemed to draw her very soul. She snaked her hands around his neck, pulling him closer. She was drowning, her legs weak with her need for him.

He pulled away. She could see that he too was shaken by the strength of their mutual desire.

'Are you sure?' he asked gently. It was all she could do to nod, then with a triumphant smile he picked her up and, holding her close in his arms, he carried her up the stairs and into their own private world.

Later, when the sun was beginning to lighten the sky, she lay on one elbow, looking down on him. Asleep he looked softer, more vulnerable somehow. He had been a passionate but considerate lover, taking his time with her, waiting until she cried out with her need to have him inside her before he took her. She smiled. Several times he had taught her things about her own body that she hadn't known. Time and time again he had brought her to a climax that had left her shuddering and almost tearful with release. She traced a finger over his lips, memorising the contours of his face, knowing she would never see him again. But it was almost all right. In one wonderful night he had managed to heal something inside her that she'd thought was beyond repair. And for that, she would never forget him.

CHAPTER TWO

ANNIE read through the case notes again to refresh her memory. Not that she needed to. She had seen Claire and Roy several times already and knew their history well. Satisfied that she was completely up to date, she sat back and waited for them to arrive.

The rain pattered depressingly against the window and Annie felt her mind drifting back to the magical last night of her Spanish holiday. Almost four months had passed and yet her memories of Raphael and the time they had spent together hadn't diminished. She could still remember his every touch, their every kiss. It was as if she had found the missing part of herself. The man she had been waiting for all her life. Her soulmate. She hadn't believed that such a person existed—but now she knew differently.

Her heart lurched. Sometimes she wished she had never met him. Because it had made being alone all the more painful, as if she'd left half of herself back in Spain. Annie sighed wistfully, remembering his last words to her.

'*Cariño*,' he had said huskily the morning she had left. 'If only you had come into my life before. But now it's too…complicated.' She hadn't pressed him to explain. What would have been the point? Still, she couldn't help trying to fathom out what he had meant. Was he married? No—she was sure if he was, his family would have made some reference to it. In love with someone else, committed in a relationship? Perhaps. But it didn't matter. Even if he had begged her to stay with him, she wouldn't have said yes. Not so soon after Robert and all their problems. No, much better to lock the memory of him in her heart. Much safer.

Annie pulled her gaze away from the window and swung her chair back round to her desk. There was no point in thinking of Raphael. She had to get on with her life. Hadn't she vowed to do just that? Besides, the irony of not being able to conceive made her a better midwife. At least she could console herself with that realisation. And her work in Penhally was more than satisfying and enjoyable. It was what got her up each morning, determined to put her own heartache behind her and help the couples who streamed through her door hoping to realise the dream that she would never have.

Like her next two patients—Roy and Claire Dickson, who were being ushered in. Annie greeted them warmly, knowing they were nervous. The couple had been trying for years to have a baby, and finally with the help of IVF had succeeded. Their initial scan had shown not one but two healthy heartbeats and now Annie, who had a special responsibility for mothers with high-risk pregnancies, was following them up regularly.

'How have you been feeling?' she asked Claire, while checking her blood pressure.

'As if I'm on cloud nine!' Claire smiled with delight. 'Apart from that, nauseous and tired and more than a little bit scared.'

'The nausea will pass. Take it as a good sign in the meantime,' Annie said.

Although she shared the couple's joy, Annie

couldn't help a pang of envy. How she would love to be in Claire's shoes, looking forward to her first babies with a loving supportive husband by her side. But she wasn't even a candidate for IVF, she thought sadly. And it wasn't as if there was a rush of people wanting to marry her either, but at least she could help this couple experience what she never could. And she found comfort in that.

'Your blood pressure is absolutely fine, but I want to keep an eye on you and these little ones. I'm sure you both know that the first twelve weeks are the riskiest.' Catching Claire's look of alarm, she hastened to reassure her. 'But you're well past that now. It's just that twin pregnancies are riskier over the whole of the pregnancy. But we are going to do everything possible to deliver two healthy babies and right now everything appears to be going fine.'

'They gave us a choice at the IVF clinic,' Roy said, as if Annie didn't already know, 'about whether we wanted one or two embryos put back. They explained the pros and cons, that there was a greater risk with twins, but we decided to take a chance and have two embryos replaced. This way we'll have a complete family in one go, and Claire doesn't have to put herself through it all again.' His grin almost split his face in two. 'I still can't believe it,' he said, patting his wife's tummy with a proprietary air. 'Two babies. Isn't she clever?'

Annie saw the happy couple to the front door of the maternity wing, and watched Claire struggling to open the umbrella over her head as she battled against the slanting rain, She was delighted for them, but it was early days yet. Twin pregnancies had a greater risk of problems developing and although that had been explained to the couple, she wondered if they really understood.

Annie felt a wave of fatigue wash over her. She always felt so caught up with her patients, sharing their see-saw emotions as she followed them through their pregnancies. Although she loved being part of the team that looked after high-risk pregnancies at St Piran Hospital, sometimes it was hard to remember that most women sailed through their pregnancies and gave birth to healthy babies without medical intervention.

But today was different and Annie knew it

wasn't just concern for her patients that was bothering her. She couldn't continue to ignore what was staring her in the face, no matter how much she wanted to. She hadn't had a period for months now and she had begun to put weight on around her middle. All the symptoms of an early menopause.

Unreasonably, even though she knew she couldn't conceive naturally, there had always been a faint glimmer of hope that one day she might have a child. No matter how much she had tried to convince herself otherwise. But with the menopause, any hope would be completely extinguished. Annie was painfully aware that she had to see someone about it, but there was only one person she really trusted and who would understand exactly how she was feeling. She would pop in to see Kate Althorp, the senior midwife at Penhally Bay Surgery, on her way home.

Annie enjoyed working with Kate and her colleague Chloe, who were both midwives based at the surgery. To begin with, they had discussed patients they shared over the phone, but over time they had become friends and Annie would often drop in at the surgery on her way home from hospital for a chat. Occasionally the three women would meet up for coffee or supper too.

Making up her mind, Annie picked up her coat. Kate would know what her next step should be. It was time for Annie to face up to whatever the future had in store. Hadn't she made that promise to herself just months before?

Annie found Kate in her office, catching up with paperwork. The older midwife looked up and smiled when she noticed Annie standing in the doorway.

'Grief, is it that time already?' She looked at her watch. 'Six o'clock! I'm due to pick Jem up from football practice in forty minutes.' She glanced back at Annie and something in Annie's expression must have alerted the experienced nurse. 'But time for some coffee before then. You look a bit peaky, methinks.'

As Kate fished out a couple of mugs, Annie wondered whether there was any point in confiding her fears. But if she was right, she would need to consider whether to start hormone replacement therapy and wanted to discuss the option with Kate before she saw Dr Nick

Tremayne, her GP and also the senior partner at the practice.

'Hey.' Kate turned and looked at her closely, her brown eyes warm with concern. 'So, what's up? Is Claire's pregnancy going okay? I know she and Roy were seeing you today.'

'Oh. No, that's fine. I intend to keep a close eye on them, but so far—touch wood—everything seems to be going as expected.'

'It's good to see them so happy. They've been waiting for this for so long. I'll call round and see Claire tomorrow,' Kate said handing a mug to Annie. 'But back to you. Something's bothering you. You didn't come here just to tell me about Claire and Roy, did you? C'mon, whatever it is, out with it.'

Annie hesitated. Once she told Kate, it would be the same as having it confirmed. Was she really ready for that?

Kate came over to Annie and dragged a chair across so she was sitting beside her. 'You don't have to tell me, but perhaps I can help?' she said gently. The older woman was always the one everyone went to with their problems. Annie wasn't sure why—perhaps because she always made time to listen and never seemed to judge. Annie felt tears sting her eyes and she blinked furiously. She wouldn't cry. She had shed enough tears to last her a lifetime.

'I never told you this, but I can't have children,' Annie blurted. 'I'm infertile.'

'Oh, Annie, I'm so sorry. Are you sure?'

'Positive,' Annie said, trying to keep her voice steady. 'You know I told you that I was seeing someone before I came back to Penhally Bay?'

Kate nodded and waited for Annie to continue.

'Robert and I were together for five years. We were in love—or so I thought. We planned to marry and started trying for a family. But after six months, when nothing had happened, I went to one of the doctors I worked with who specialised in infertility and he suggested we get tested. There was nothing wrong with Robert but they have a new blood test that they use to check a woman's fertility. Well, the result came back. My ovarian reserve, you know the number of eggs I have left, was so low as to be immeasurable.' Annie's voice broke. She remembered the day she had been given the news as if it were yesterday.

Kate put her arm around Annie's shoulder. Her silent sympathy gave Annie the strength to continue. 'The test is very reliable. A pregnancy, even with IVF, would be almost impossible for me. They also warned me that it was likely that I would have an early menopause.' She steadied her voice. 'Well, I think it's happening,' she said, trying not to show how much it hurt her to say the words. 'I haven't had a period since…' She thought back. 'Well, before New Year. And,' she continued, 'I don't know how else to describe this, but I kind of feel all hormonal, as if my emotions are all over the place. You know it took me all my willpower not to cry when I saw how relieved and happy Claire and Roy are, and that's not like me. Not that I don't care about them, of course I do, but I don't usually let it get to me like this.'

'But it's understandable, isn't it?' Kate said softly. 'It's bound to remind you of your own loss. And losing the ability to have a family is a loss. Just as much as a death.'

'I know all that,' Annie said, 'but I've been feeling so much happier since I came back from Spain. When I was over there, I knew I had to stop looking back and try and think positively about the future. Accept that children weren't on the cards for me and make something of my life. Be happy with what I have, instead of hankering for what can never be. But if I'm right and I'm experiencing the onset of the menopause, it's like having to deal with it all over again.'

'And you are certain that that's what's happening?' Kate said thoughtfully.

'There can't be another explanation. Missed periods. Emotions all over the place, and I swear I'm starting a middle-age spread. I could hardly get into my jeans the other day.' Annie tried a smile.

Kate looked at her sharply. 'All this since your holiday? Hmm. I don't suppose you had a holiday romance while you were away?'

Annie felt a blush creep up her cheeks. Seeing it, Kate grinned. 'You did, didn't you? Well, good for you. It's about time you let yourself have some fun.' Then she frowned. 'If it was fun. Oh, dear, I didn't mean for it to come out that way. You know what I mean.'

Annie felt her blush deepen as she thought

back to that night. Fun? Yes, but now one of her most precious memories.

'And, if you had sex, did you use contraception?' That was typical Kate. Straight to the point.

'Yes, I mean…no.' Annie blushed again. 'I mean, I told him it wasn't necessary and he just assumed I was on the Pill.' Oh, dear, this was so embarrassing. Although she felt comfortable discussing most things with Kate, there really was a limit.

'What I'm getting at,' Kate said gently, still looking thoughtful. 'I don't suppose you've taken a pregnancy test?'

Annie was stunned. A pregnancy test! The thought simply hadn't occurred to her. She had accepted that it was impossible, so hadn't even considered it. Not even for a second.

'Well, no. It's hardly likely is it? Not with my history.' Suddenly she felt dizzy. 'You don't think? It couldn't be? Could it?' Although she knew it was impossible, the sudden leap of hope was almost too much to bear.

Kate stood up, all business. 'It wouldn't hurt to make sure, would it? Come on.' She rooted around in a cupboard. 'Off you go to the Ladies and produce a specimen and we'll do a quick test. At the very least we'll be able to rule it out.'

Ten minutes later, Annie was sitting stunned in front of Kate. 'You're sure?' she said. 'There couldn't be some mistake?'

'I'm sure,' Kate replied smiling widely. 'We'll arrange a scan just to be absolutely certain, but there is no doubt in my mind. You are pregnant. Apart from the test, I could feel something when I palpated your tummy. I've seen it happen before. Just when a woman thinks a baby is out of the question. Then bam.'

Annie felt a wave of pure joy suffuse her soul. A baby! She was going to have a baby. She had longed for this moment for so long, and now it was here, she could hardly bring herself to believe it. Now the tiredness, the roller-coaster emotions, the hormonal mood swings all made perfect sense. She hugged herself, barely able to contain her delight.

'I assume you're not still in touch with the father? I mean, you've never mentioned him,' Kate was saying.

Raphael! Of course it must be his. He was the only man she had slept with since Robert.

'No. I haven't spoken to him since, well, you know.' How *would* Raphael feel about it? Was there any point in telling him? She neither expected nor wanted anything from him and his silence had made it perfectly clear that he wanted nothing from her, either. Her head reeled. She would have to take time off work, of course, at least for the first few months after the birth, but she had a small inheritance from her grandfather that would supplement her maternity pay. One way or another she would cope. One thing was for sure—her baby wouldn't be short of love.

'God, should I tell him? I don't know. I'm still trying to take it all in. I can hardly believe it myself. But I suppose he has the right to know.'

Annie thought she saw something move behind Kate's eyes, but almost as quickly it was gone. She knew Kate had brought up her child, Jem, on her own since the death of her husband, James. Although it must have been a struggle, Kate had had no choice. James had died before he had even known she was pregnant. All this must be bringing back painful memories for the older woman.

'Only you can make that decision,' Kate replied gently. 'Whatever is right for you.'

'I don't know if I want him in my life, Kate. It's a complication I could do without. Besides, he lives in Spain. Even if he wants to get to know his child, it won't be easy.'

Once again, Annie thought she saw a shadow cross Kate's face, but Annie knew her friend well enough not to ask. Although always willing to offer guidance and support, Kate rarely discussed her own personal life.

'As I said, it's up to you,' Kate said. 'But if you don't tell him, what will you say to your child when he asks about his father?'

Instinctively, Annie knew Kate was right. Whatever the consequences, telling Raphael was the right thing to do, even if he then wanted nothing to do with the baby. One day her child might want to seek out his father. How could she tell the child that its father didn't even know they existed? And if Raphael wanted contact, it wouldn't be right to deny her child the opportunity to know his father. But she had so much to think about right now, the decision could wait. The important thing was that she, Annie Thomas, ordinary woman with an ordinary life, had had this extra-ordinary thing happen to her.

And for that alone she would always be grateful to Dr Raphael Castillo.

After Kate had seen a deliriously happy Annie out, she sat deep in thought. She remembered the day she had found out she was pregnant with Jem. A day infused with happiness but also regret and profound sadness. Her son had been conceived the night she had lost her husband to the first big storm almost eleven years ago. But Jem hadn't been her husband's child. While James had been out there fighting for his life, she had been in the arms of senior partner Nick Tremayne, and the guilt had haunted her every day since. She hadn't been able to tell Nick that Jem was his when she'd found out she was pregnant. It wouldn't have been fair. He had still been married to Annabel with children of his own, but he had found out the truth anyway and in the worst possible way when he had overheard her telling pathologist Eloise Haydon.

Kate rose and went across to the window. It was dark outside and the glass pane reflected back her blurred image, softening the faint lines that had started to appear around her eyes. Although she was no longer in her first bloom of youth, she still remembered in minute detail the passion her younger self had felt all these years ago, and, if she was honest with herself, the feelings had never truly faded.

What if she had told Nick that Jem was his as soon as she had found out? Would he have accepted Jem as his child then? But it was no use thinking like that. Rightly or wrongly she had made her decision and had lived with the consequences. Now Annie had to make up her own mind whether to tell the father of *her* child. Kate just hoped that her story would have a different outcome from hers.

After leaving Kate, Annie had spent the rest of the night telephoning her parents and siblings with her exciting news.

'Oh, darling, that's wonderful news!' her mother had said. 'I can only imagine how delighted you must be. I can't wait to tell Dad and David. They're all down at the beach at the moment with the children.'

Annie had felt a pang. She would have loved to share her news face to face with her family. Instead, they were thousands of miles away.

'Do you want us to come back?' her mother had added anxiously.

'Of course not, Mum. I know how long you and Dad have been looking forward to this trip. Anyway, you'll be back in August. In plenty of time for the actual birth.'

There had been silence for a few moments.

'Does that mean you and Robert are back together?' her mother asked. Annie could hear the caution in her voice. She had never really taken to Robert and when he had left Annie after hearing she couldn't have children, she had admitted as much to her daughter. 'Any man who behaves the way he did isn't worthy of you, darling,' she had said. 'You are better off without him.'

Annie knew she'd be thinking back to her words.

'It's not Robert's baby,' Annie said quietly. Once again the silence stretched down the phone line. Annie knew her mother was dying to know who the father was, but wouldn't ask.

'The father is someone I met in Spain—a doctor,' Annie said uncomfortably. 'Not someone I'll ever see again.' She felt her toes curl with embarrassment. How could she possibly explain to anyone, even her mother, about Raphael? How he had made her feel as if they were meant to be together? And how hopelessly wrong she had been?

'As long as you're happy, darling,' her mother had said finally, gently and without judgement. 'And you won't be alone. Dad and I will be back to help you with the baby.' After a few more minutes of conversation Annie had rung off and phoned her sister Fiona. The conversation had followed a similar pattern except Fi, while thrilled for her, had in typical fashion come straight to the point.

'Does your Dr Castillo know?'

It was a timely reminder to Annie that there was more than her involved in the life growing joyously inside her.

'Not yet,' Annie admitted. 'I'm planning to tcll him, but…' She let the words tail off. It wasn't a conversation she was looking forward to, especially over the phone. There was no way of knowing what his reaction would be. He would be shocked, but would he be pleased? Angry? Disinterested?

'But you will tell him,' Fi prompted. 'You know it's the right thing to do.'

'Yes,' Annie replied heavily. 'And we both know I always do the right thing.'

But she had kept putting the telephone call off. She hadn't spoken to Raphael since the morning she had left Spain, although she thought of him often, hugging the memory of the night they had spent together. If she was honest, she had hoped he would get in touch with her. There had been such a connection between them, she just couldn't believe he hadn't felt it too. But if he had, he would have found a way to contact her, wouldn't he? But he hadn't and Annie had resigned herself to never hearing from him, concentrating instead on making a life for herself that was rich and varied and relied on no one.

After a couple of days of prevaricating, she made up her mind. She looked up the number of the hospital in Barcelona and, after taking a few deep breaths to calm her nerves, dialled and asked to be put through to Dr Castillo.

As she waited for the switchboard to page him, her heart thumped painfully. How would he take the news? It was bound to be a shock, however he felt about it. When they had made love, she had told him that there was no need for contraception, although she hadn't told him why.

She chewed on her nail until suddenly she heard his unmistakable voice on the other end of the phone.

'*Hola!* Raphael Castillo.'

Immediately memories came flooding back. She could see his face in her mind, almost feel the touch of his fingers on her skin.

Her hands were shaking so hard she thought she might drop the phone. 'Raphael, it's Annie.' There was a long pause on the other end of the line. Whether it was because he couldn't remember who she was or because he was shocked to hear from her, she couldn't tell.

'How are you? Is something wrong? ' His voice sounded cautious.

'No, nothing's wrong. At least…' She let the words hang in the air. Nothing was wrong as far as she was concerned, but how would he feel? 'I'm sorry to call you at the hospital, Raphael, but I didn't know how else to contact you.'

'*De nada,*' he said. 'Please, go on.' He sounded

brusque, almost distracted, as if speaking to Annie had been the last thing on his mind. She couldn't help the way her spirits dipped. How could she expect anything else? If he had wanted to get in touch with her before now, well, he knew where she worked. That night obviously hadn't meant as much to him as it had to her, but it didn't matter, she told herself firmly. She didn't need him. She had all she ever wanted growing inside her.

All of a sudden she couldn't remember the words she had rehearsed, but she knew she had to say something as he was waiting for her to speak.

'I'm pregnant,' she blurted finally, not at all how she had planned to tell him.

There was another pause, longer this time.

'Pregnant? I thought you said…'

'That I couldn't get pregnant,' she finished for him. She had told him it was safe for them to have sex. He had assumed she was on the Pill and there had been no point in disabusing him.

'I didn't think it could happen, but it did!' She couldn't keep the joy out of her voice. Every time she said the words she felt a fresh burst of happiness.

When he spoke again his voice was cold. 'Is it mine?'

Annie reeled. What was he suggesting? That she was passing off some other man's child as his? Or that she slept with so many men she couldn't possibly know which one was the father? She felt the first stirring of anger.

'Yes, it's yours. It couldn't be anyone else's. You were the only man…' She hesitated, feeling a blush steal up her cheeks. It was so difficult to talk about this over the phone. At least he couldn't see how mortified she was. 'You are the only man I've slept with since…' Once more she stumbled over the words. 'It can only be yours.'

Another long silence. Why hadn't she just written to him? It would have been so much easier. But she had never been one to take the easy way out.

'You must be over three months by now in that case,' he said slowly. The pause must have been while he had worked the timing out in his head. 'Why didn't you let me know sooner? I'm assuming you're going to keep it.' His voice was cool. He seemed so utterly different from the man she had met in Spain.

'Of course I'm going to keep it! I would hardly be telling you now if I wasn't. I've only recently found out myself.' She stumbled over the words. 'Just a few days ago, but...' She took a deep breath. How could she explain the conflicting thoughts she had had about telling him? 'I just didn't realise I was pregnant. It didn't occur to me that I could be before then.' She could only imagine what he was thinking. How could a midwife not know she was pregnant? But she didn't really want to get into her medical history over the phone. As far as she was concerned, she had done her duty in telling him.

'And?' His voice was heavy, almost suspicious. 'Why exactly are you telling me now? What do you want from me?'

Annie felt a wave of anger wash over her. She hadn't expected him to be pleased, but this reaction, as if he didn't believe or trust her, as if she had ulterior motives for contacting him, wasn't what she had expected either.

'I'm just phoning to let you know. I thought you had a right.' She laughed but the sound was mirthless even to her own ears. 'But don't worry, I don't want anything from you. Not a thing. In fact, I want to be clear that this baby is my responsibility and mine alone,' she continued. 'I don't intend to keep secrets from my child. I plan to be honest about everything from as soon as they can understand. It might be that one day, when they are older, he or she may want to find you. That's why I'm telling you. No other reason.'

'*If* it is my baby—' he emphasised the first word '—then, of course, you were right to tell me. But how can I be sure?'

Annie felt as if she'd been slapped. But to be fair he wasn't to know she didn't make a habit of sleeping with strangers, especially not men she met on holiday. She took another breath to calm herself.

'It's yours. There is absolutely no doubt. But if you don't want to accept that, it's entirely up to you. I have done my bit. I'll say goodbye now.'

She thought she heard him say, 'Wait, Annie,' as she replaced the receiver, but she was in no mood to continue the discussion. As far as she was concerned, Raphael would play no part in her or her baby's life. And that was fine by her.

* * *

Raphael replaced the phone thoughtfully. It had been a shock hearing Annie's voice after all these months. He remembered every cadence of her soft accent and as soon as he had heard her speak, it had been as if she had been back in his arms.

It wasn't as if he hadn't thought about her every day since the night they had met. He hadn't been able to get her striking pale green eyes out of his mind, her wounded mouth, her pale skin a striking contrast to her luxurious dark brown hair and that deep but unmistakable air of sadness. How could he forget the curve of her hips, the sweep of her thighs, her tiny waist? He groaned aloud at the memory. He had done his best to put her out of his mind, and now, when he least expected it, she was back in his life. Because she was pregnant. With his baby. Or so she said.

He started pacing. There was no reason for Annie to lie about such a thing and she had made it perfectly clear that she wanted nothing from him. But he had been lied to before and he knew he couldn't trust his heart. It was why he had stayed away from her in the first place, even when every part of him had longed to be with her again.

He swore under his breath. If she was lying, he would find out. But if there was any chance she was carrying his child, any chance at all…

He clenched his jaw against the painful memory of Sebastian. *Dios!* This time no one was going to take his child from him. He had to know the truth and there was only one way to find out.

CHAPTER THREE

OVER the next week, Annie mulled over her conversation with Raphael. She wondered if there had been any point in telling him she was pregnant. It might have been the right thing to do, but it had obviously made no difference. She hadn't heard a peep from him since the call and that was fine by her. What he chose to do with the information was up to him.

Nevertheless, she couldn't help acknowledge that she felt sad about his response. Not for herself, but for the child growing inside her. One day, he—or she—might want to know about their father and she would have to find a way of telling her child that his father had shown no interest.

Everyone at work knew about her pregnancy and it was all Annie could do to stop herself accosting strangers in the street and telling them that she was expecting a baby. She was so happy she wanted to shout it from the rooftops. But as far as who the father was, that would be her secret. Somehow explaining about Raphael would make it sound like a casual fling—when it had been anything but. Besides, as he had shown no interest, there was no reason for anyone, apart from her immediate family, to know his identity. She would bc raising this child on her own and that was fine by her.

Annie chewed her lip. She looked around her tiny home with its double bedroom, minute single bedroom, kitchen and lounge. She loved it. It was so cosy, especially in the winter when she would light a fire and cuddle up on the sofa with a good book, but it wasn't really big enough for her and a baby. The second bedroom would only just be large enough for a cot and a changing table. However, it would have to do. Despite the small inheritance from her grandfather, money was bound to be tight after her maternity pay came to an end. But what did money or any material possessions matter when balanced against having a baby?

It didn't. She would have happily given up everything she owned if she'd had to just to be in this position.

A knock on the door interrupted her thoughts. Annie wasn't expecting anyone. Sunday was a day that everyone she knew spent with their families. Puzzled, she opened the door to find the last person she expected standing there, a half-smile on his face.

Raphael! It couldn't be! What on earth was he doing here, in Penhally Bay? And why did her heart feel as if it had stopped beating?

Speechless, Annie stood aside to let him enter, and as he passed her she felt her skin prickle. Her breath caught in her throat as instantly she was transported back to the night she had spent in his arms.

She waved at a chair, still unable to speak, but he shook his head. Instead, he paced her small house with nervous energy.

'I had to come,' he said simply.

'Why?' she said, dry-mouthed. 'I told you there was no need.'

'Because if there is a chance you are having my baby,' he said, sounding incredulous, 'I want to be here for him. He will need a father. I don't even know if you can look after a child.'

Annie felt her temper rise. Just who did he think he was, coming here to check up on her, questioning not only her morals but her ability to look after *her* child?

'Believe me, I am having *your* baby, and I'm perfectly able to look after it by myself. I certainly didn't expect you to come charging over here like a knight on a white horse.'

'But now I am here to find out if it is really mine.'

Annie swallowed, forcing herself to stay calm. 'You have to make up your own mind whether you believe me or not—although I can't think why you imagine I'm lying to you. As far as I'm concerned, I've told you. What you do with the information is up to you.'

He looked at her with flat eyes.

'You told me it was safe for us to have sex. Why did you tell me that if it wasn't true?'

'I thought it was safe. I never dreamt I could fall pregnant,' Annie replied, trying to keep her voice even. 'Look, I don't care whether you believe me or not. I'm not asking anything from you, so you are hardly in a position to demand proof from me!'

Suddenly the tension left Raphael's face. He grinned, the lopsided smile reminding Annie once again of the man she had met back in Spain.

'Please forgive me. I didn't come to make you angry with me. I want to believe it is mine and as long as there is that chance, I'm staying. Right here. In Penhally Bay.'

'You're staying here?' Annie said incredulously. 'But what about your job back in Spain?'

Raphael shrugged. 'I managed to persuade them to give me a six-month sabbatical. And I have a post for that time in the hospital at St Piran.' He nodded in the vague direction of the hospital a good thirty minutes up the road.

'You have a job? At St. Piran's?' Annie was only too aware that she was repeating his words parrot fashion. But it was all such a shock. At the very most, she'd imagined her staying in touch with him by phone, at least until the baby was born. Then the odd visit. But it seemed she had totally underestimated the man.

'How on earth did you manage to get a job at the hospital so soon? I only phoned you last week.'

'I know many people,' he said. 'I have many connections through my work. In the end it was not too difficult.' He smiled, a flash of white against his bronzed skin. 'And I specialise in high-risk pregnancies. So they were happy to have me on their team.'

Annie sat down in the chair. He could stand if he liked, but she needed something more solid to support her legs, which seemed to have turned to rubber again. He specialised in high-risk pregnancies. That meant they'd be working together. Every day.

'I need to know everything is all right with the baby,' he continued. 'You must be in your second trimester by now. Have you had a scan? Is everything normal? Have you been taking folic acid?' He fired the questions at Annie as if he were an interrogating officer of a hostile army.

'Perhaps you'd like to know what size feet I have while you're at it,' Annie muttered under her breath. Whatever he said, these weren't the questions of a man who doubted that he was the father. Suddenly she relented. He was here now and he was entitled to know how her pregnancy was progressing.

'Please, Raphael, sit down,' Annie said quietly. She couldn't think straight while he was prowling around her like a lion circling its prey. For once he did as she asked and sat down in her armchair, still eyeing her warily.

'Everything is normal, and, yes, I have had a scan.' She stood up, relieved to find that her legs could support her, crossed over to her bookshelf and pulled out the photograph of her scan. Silently she passed it over to him.

She watched as Raphael studied the photograph carefully. A kaleidoscope of emotions crossed his face ranging from awe to intense interest. Then he looked at her and it was if the shutters came down.

'Good,' he said flatly. 'Everything looks as it should. Is it a boy or a girl?'

Annie hid a smile. He seemed determined not to show her how affected he was, but pride—or was it possessiveness?—was written all over his face. Suddenly she felt uneasy.

'I don't know the sex,' she said. 'I want it to be a surprise. Look, Raphael, if you wanted to check up on how the pregnancy was going, you could have phoned me, come for a visit even, but from what you've told me, you're planning to stick around. For the next six months at least.'

'If it is my child,' he said, 'then it needs a father as well as a mother. I don't have to stay here, you can come back with me to Spain. It will be better. You can stop work, stay with my family.'

Annie shook her head, dismayed. 'You can't be serious.' She gave a small laugh. 'Why on earth would I want to do that? My life is here. My job, my friends, my family. My baby will be born here and live here. We don't need you to support us. Is that the reason you think I called? So you would come running with financial support?'

Annie was trying hard to keep her tone even. Just who did he think he was to come barging back into her life? Hadn't she made her position perfectly clear?

Suddenly Raphael looked contrite. 'I am sorry,' he said. 'I came in here like a bull in a...how do you say? Field? Shop?'

'China shop,' Annie answered automatically.

'Whatever. Forgive me?' he said, the boyish grin back on his face. 'It is just that I too want this child very much. I have to be part of his life. Can you understand?'

'Yes. Of course. It's just that I wasn't expecting you to come rushing over here, taking a job. Speaking of which, what happens after your job comes to an end?'

'Oh, I will not go back to Spain—not until I can take my child with me. Until then, I will stay here. It is settled.'

'You plan to live here? Permanently?' Annie said shocked. Whatever she had been expecting, it wasn't this.

Raphael crossed his arms across his chest and nodded emphatically. 'If I have to.'

'I suppose I can't stop you,' Annie said slowly. 'But I want to make one thing clear—this baby is my responsibility.'

'And mine.' His mouth was set in a determined line.

'I am happy to be on my own. I don't want any thing from you—least of all a relationship. Although I guess the fact that you never tried to contact me means that it was never an option as far as you were concerned, either.'

Raphael narrowed his eyes at her. 'We never

made any promises, either of us. There were things…' He paused, shaking his head. 'It just couldn't be.'

He was right, of course. There hadn't been any promises on either side, but that hadn't stopped her hoping he would get in touch, even while she knew she had nothing to offer him.

'Where will you live?' Annie asked, dragging her thoughts back to the present.

'I have taken a room in a hotel near the hospital for the time being, but I will look for a place here in Penhally Bay. I want to keep an eye on you and the pregnancy.'

Annie's thoughts were all over the place. He was here and if that wasn't a big enough shock, he was planning to stay.

'I should tell you that I have consulted a lawyer, in Spain as well as in the UK. I'm going to ask for shared access. No one is going to stop me seeing my child.'

Annie looked at him, aghast. Her growing feeling of unease was spot on. He was here and determined to interfere with her life. It was one thing letting him know he was going to be a father, quite another him demanding legal access. Too late, the memory of the words he had spoken in Spain came rushing back. 'If she were my child,' he had said referring to Maria, 'nothing and no one would stop me claiming what belongs to me.' At the time his words had meant little but now they burnt into her brain, sending a frisson of fear down her spine. What on earth had she done? And what could she do about it now?

CHAPTER FOUR

ANNIE studied the CTG of the pregnant woman whose labour she was monitoring for the umpteenth time. Although the contractions were still several minutes apart, the baby's heartbeat kept slowing down. Over the last couple of hours it had returned to normal within a few seconds, but this time the baby's heart rate stayed slow. The baby was clearly in distress and Annie knew that the mother should be delivered right now. Making up her mind, she asked one of the staff midwives to page the on-call consultant and let them know they were needed straight away.

While she waited, Annie explained to her patient that it was likely she would need to have a C-section.

Audrey looked at her with frightened eyes. 'I really wanted a natural birth,' she said.

'I know you did,' Annie said softly. She had been involved with Audrey's pregnancy all the way through and had helped her put a birth plan together.

'But sometimes things don't turn out the way we'd hoped. This is the best for your baby. And that's what's important in the end, isn't it? We should be able to give you a spinal, so at least you'll be awake to welcome your child into the world.'

Audrey sought her husband's hand. 'Of course you're right. All that matters is that my baby is okay.' She grimaced as another contraction hit her. 'I trust you to decide what's right for us,' she told Annie once the wave of pain had passed.

During the contraction, Annie had been watching the baby's heartbeat on the monitor. As before, it slowed down, but this time it was almost three minutes before the heart rate returned to normal. Where was the obstetrician? She tried to remember who was on call for labour ward, but couldn't. There had been so many changes recently with people going on leave, it was hard to keep up

Just as she was about to ask Julie, her fellow

midwife, to call the consultant again, Raphael strode into the room.

'Someone paged me,' he said, seemingly oblivious to the fact that Annie was in the room. Although she had known she'd bump into him sooner rather than later, she was unprepared for the way her heart started pounding in her chest.

'It was me, Dr Castillo,' Annie said, thankful her voice didn't betray the unsteady beating of her heart. 'Audrey's baby is having repeated prolonged decelerations. She's only 5 cms. I think we need to get her delivered straight away.' She handed the CTG printout to Raphael, who studied it for a few moments before nodding.

'You're absolutely right,' he said. 'We need to get Audrey to theatre straight away. Could someone let the anaesthetist know we need him to do a spinal? Come on, let's get going.' As everyone reacted to his words, he bent over Audrey. 'Try not to worry. We'll have your baby out and in your arms shortly.'

There wasn't time in the next few minutes for Annie to think about anything except her patient. Quickly she and Julie, with a few words of reassurance to Audrey and her husband, started wheeling the bed down to theatre. Minutes later, Annie was washing her hands next to Raphael while he scrubbed up.

'Excellent call,' he said approvingly. 'It's good that you didn't wait any longer before calling me.'

'I have been a midwife for several years, Dr Castillo.'

Raphael arched an eyebrow but said nothing. Annie followed him into theatre.

Annie stood back ready to receive Audrey's baby while Raphael, after checking with the anaesthetist that Audrey's lower body was suitably numb, cut into the abdomen and then into the uterus. They all waited with bated breath as he pulled out the baby. There was a second of complete stillness before a lusty cry of rage broke the silence. Everyone smiled. Raphael passed the baby across to Annie who promptly wrapped it in a blanket before checking that the airway was clear.

'You have a beautiful baby boy,' she said to Audrey, passing her the newborn to hold. 'And he's absolutely perfect.'

While Raphael was suturing the wound in Audrey's abdomen, Annie, a lump in her throat, watched as Audrey and her husband cooed over their son. No matter how many times she delivered a baby, it always got to her, but for the first time in as long as she could remember there was no stab of envy as she watched a mother with her baby. In a few months' time, she would be holding a child of her own.

Glancing up from the happy trio, she found Raphael's speculative eyes on hers and wondered if he was thinking the same thing.

'We'll get you up to recovery as soon as Dr Castillo has finished closing,' she told Audrey. 'I'm just going to weigh your son and then I'll give him right back to you. Then you can try giving him a feed.' As soon as she finished checking the baby over, she passed him back to Audrey, and helped her settle her son onto the breast. Happily the tiny infant got the hang of it straight away and was soon sucking contentedly. Annie felt her throat constrict. Damn the tears that were never far away these days. At least these were the right kind of tears.

As soon as she had settled mother and baby in the postnatal ward, she headed off to the staff room. She needed to find a place where she could be alone with her thoughts. How on earth was she going to cope over the next few months, seeing Raphael every day? Yesterday she had asked him to leave, promising that they would talk again, but what could she say to him? That she had never stopped thinking about him and the night they had shared together? That it had taken all her willpower not to call him and that seeing him again had made her greedy for more? That suddenly she wanted it all—a child, yes, but also someone who loved them…both. But she knew that wasn't going to happen. If that night had meant anything at all he would have found her before now, despite what they had told each other.

As she tried to concentrate on her paperwork she became aware of someone watching her. She looked up to find Raphael studying her with an odd expression in his eyes.

'*Hola,*' he said softly. 'Can I come in?'

'It's not really a good time. I have to finish this paperwork before my afternoon clinic.'

He ignored her and, frowning, stepped into the room. 'When, then?' he demanded. 'When would be a good time? Because you and I need to talk about this baby,' he said. A muscle twitched in his cheek. He wasn't quite as casual as he had first seemed.

'I'm not sure that there's anything left to talk about,' Annie said. Then she relented. It had been a shock seeing him again, but now he was here, and she would be working closely with him over the coming months, she could hardly ignore him.

'Look,' she said. 'Why don't you come over this evening? Around seven? We can talk then, okay?'

He crossed the room and leaned over the table, his brown eyes drilling into hers. Annie felt like a moth trapped in a light and it was all she could do to stop herself from leaping up and moving away. Somehow she found the resolve to return his look steadily. He searched her face for a moment.

'Okay,' he said. 'Until tonight.' And, turning on his heel, he was gone.

As soon as Annie got home, she rushed around tidying up before jumping in the shower. As she soaped her body, she felt the small burgeoning lump of her pregnancy under her fingers and smiled. Then, as she let the hot water ease away the tiredness, her thoughts focused on Raphael.

How would she cope, seeing him every day? Especially when the rapid beating of her heart every time she looked at him told her that the connection she had felt with him in Spain was still there. It hadn't just been the Mediterranean sun after all, though she had always known it had been much more than that.

Finishing her shower, she went to slip on a pair of jeans, but to her dismay, and secret delight, she couldn't do up the button. It was time to go shopping for some maternity clothes. She hadn't allowed herself to think that far ahead until now. A little suspicious side of her was afraid of tempting fate. She discarded the too-tight jeans in favour of a simple dress. Then she brushed her long dark hair until it shone, before adding a touch of eye shadow and lipstick. She refused to ask herself why she was taking so much time with her appearance.

The late spring evening was unseasonably warm, so she opened the window and the smell of her climbing roses floated in on the breeze. Should she offer him a meal? she wondered. What was the polite way to behave when meeting the father of your child after a one-night stand? Once again, she felt her face grow warm at the memory. She thought about phoning Fiona to tell her Raphael had turned up, and asking her for advice, but before she had the chance, there was a knock on her door. She felt a tingle of apprehension dance up her spine as she opened the door.

Raphael stood in the doorway, holding a bunch of tulips. She couldn't read the expression on his face, and before she could say anything, he handed her the flowers.

'Thank you,' she said simply, burying her nose in their fragrance. 'They're lovely.' She stood aside to let him enter. Once again she was dismayed at the way her heart was thumping.

'I thought we could go for a walk,' Annie said, feeling the need for neutral territory. 'I could show you Penhally Bay.'

'I would like that.'

Annie draped a sweater over her shoulders and soon they were following the road down to the harbour.

'How are your family?' she asked. 'And little Maria? I have thought of her often.'

'They are all well. Maria asks after the British

woman with the sad green eyes often.' He stopped and turned towards her. 'But you don't look so sad to me any more.' He traced a finger down the line of her jaw. 'You look happy.'

'I am. Very happy.'

They continued following the road until they came to the lighthouse. They stood looking across the harbour to the sea beyond.

'It's hard to believe right now, when everything is so calm, but there was a bad storm here,' Annie said. 'It caused a lot of damage and there are still a lot of repairs being carried out to some of the buildings. A couple of people lost their lives. It's a small community and everybody feels it when something so awful happens.'

'It must have been hard on everyone. It is like this where my mother lives in Spain. Everybody knows and helps each other. It is a good way to live.'

'It's quiet now,' Annie continued. 'But you wouldn't believe how busy it gets in the summer months. I love it here.'

'In my country, we are always outdoors.' Raphael stopped and looked at her intently. 'It is a good country for a child to live. They can be outside playing instead of inside playing computer games, like so many of the children in this country.'

It seemed their walk was just another opportunity for Raphael to try and convince her to come and live in Spain, she thought, unable to prevent a stab of disappointment. Couldn't he see it was out of the question?

'Children here in Penhally Bay have a good life too,' she said. 'Many of them surf or sail, and there's always the beach for the younger ones. I loved it here when I was a child. It is a good place, a safe place for children. The community looks out for each other. Admittedly it attracts thousands of tourists in the summer, but that is a good thing too. It means that there is plenty going on for teenagers as well as adults. We have a very low crime rate here.'

'It is beautiful,' Raphael admitted, his eyes sweeping the bay. 'Almost as beautiful as where I live. But the weather.' He spread his hands. 'It is cold. And the rain. In Spain, there is always family around. The children spend time with their grandparents and aunts and uncles as well as cousins. Like you say, there are always people to watch out.'

They carried on walking, falling into step alongside each other. 'What about your family?' he asked. 'Don't you mind being far away from them?'

'I go to see my parents and my sister often and sometimes they come here. I'd always planned go to Australia to see my brother and his family, but I guess I'll have to shelve that plan for a while.' She smiled, thinking of the reason a visit to Australia would be out of the question for some time. 'We lived in Penhally Bay until I was about seven, when we moved to Edinburgh, so it always felt like a second home.'

'Why did you come back? Did you not like Edinburgh?'

'I'm not really a city girl. I love being able to open my front door and let the sea air in. I love the way everyone knows everyone else here— even if it does mean people know more about your business than you'd like.'

She slid a glance at him, wondering if he realised that the pair of them were bound to become a source of gossip. Not that it would be malicious, but people were bound to speculate eventually about the pregnant midwife and the Spanish doctor.

'So, they will talk about us,' Raphael said, shrugging his shoulders. 'It is of no importance. I am not ashamed.'

'Look, Raphael, can we talk about why you're here?' Annie was panting slightly as she spoke. Raphael placed a hand on her arm, indicating a bench with a tip of his dark head and leading her towards it.

They sat in silence for a few minutes, watching the surfers out at sea. The waves were a decent size and a number of people were making the most of it.

'You told me you've spoken to the lawyers about access. You didn't need to do that. I wouldn't stop you from seeing your child, not as long as you came to see him when you were supposed to. The only thing I don't want is a father who flits in and out of my child's life. A father who can't be depended on. I would much rather you have no involvement than that. But it scares me that you are consulting lawyers. I don't really understand why you seem to feel the need. I would have done anything to have a child. The last thing I would do is to take it away from you.'

Raphael brought his eyebrows together. 'Is that what happened, Annie? You wanted a child and you used me to have one?'

'It wasn't like that!' Annie insisted. 'You don't understand…'

He turned cool brown eyes on her. 'What is there to understand? You have what you want,' he said. 'Now I will have what is mine.'

Annie shivered. There was no mistaking the determination in the set of his mouth.

'In which case,' she replied, 'if that is what you think of me, I don't think there is anything left to say.'

She stood, leaving him sitting there staring out to sea.

CHAPTER FIVE

OVER the next week Annie kept bumping into Raphael but apart from his pointed enquiries into how she was feeling, their contact was limited to clinical discussions. When she saw him with his patients she was struck by his easygoing manner and they all seemed to love the way he managed to achieve the right balance between casual joking and interested concern. However, when he looked at her, his expression turned cool.

And it wasn't just the patients. He was causing quite a stir among the other female members of staff too. Annie was constantly overhearing conversations speculating about whether Dr Castillo was involved with anyone. Thankfully no one guessed that Annie and Raphael had met before, let alone that she was carrying his baby.

Annie was looking forward to a couple of days

off over the weekend. She loved her job, but she hadn't been sleeping well the last few nights. Not since Raphael had turned up, in fact, and she was longing for an early night in bed with a good book.

She only had one more patient to see before she called it a day. Morgan was an anxious-looking woman who had come for her first antenatal appointment. She had taken a home pregnancy test and estimated she was about eight weeks pregnant.

'We'll just do another one here,' Annie said. 'If that's okay with you?'

'Is that necessary? I mean, there's no doubt I'm pregnant. The test was positive and my breasts are tender and I've even developed a bump already.' She dropped her hand to her stomach, a dreamy smile on her face. But there was something that was sending alarm bells ringing for Annie. She couldn't quite put her finger on it, but she knew she'd be happier when she repeated the test herself.

When she looked at the stick, she knew that her instincts had been correct. The test was negative. Not even the faintest blue line. Her heart sank. She hated days like these when she had to be the bearer of bad news. If Morgan had been pregnant, she wasn't any longer. Just to make absolutely sure, Annie decided to ask Raphael to come and see her.

Morgan must have seen the look on her face when she came back into the room. Her face puckered.

'I am so sorry,' Annie said gently. 'But the test is negative.' She could feel every word pierce the woman like an arrow.

'But I have to be! I've wanted this for so long. And I have all the symptoms. Your test must be wrong.'

'I don't think it is, but just in case, I'm going to ask Dr Castillo to scan you. He has the most experience of scanning women in early pregnancy.'

Morgan started to cry and Annie's heart went out to her. She paged Raphael, hoping that he hadn't left for the day. She was relieved when he answered, and when she told him about her concerns he said that he would come immediately.

Annie had only enough time to prepare her patient for the scan when Raphael arrived. As usual he looked breathtakingly handsome, but Annie, still reeling from his revelation about consulting a lawyer, told herself that she couldn't care less how he looked. Any man who suggested that she had used him to get pregnant and in the same breath threatened to take her child from her wasn't a man she wanted anything to do with. How she could have fooled herself into thinking that they were some kind of kindred spirits was beyond her. And if he made her heart tumble every time she saw him, that was just physical attraction and she would get over it.

Annie brought him up to speed and Raphael took Morgan by the hand and looked into her eyes.

'I am just going to have a look at your uterus,' he said softly. 'If there is a baby in there, I will find it. Have you had any bleeding?' Morgan shook her head silently.

Raphael waited while Annie squirted some ultrasound gel on Morgan's belly. Then he glided the probe over her tummy while watching the monitor intently. Finally he shook his head.

'I'm sorry, but there is no baby there. In

fact, there is no evidence you have been pregnant recently.'

'But I am,' Morgan wailed. 'Please look again. It must be there. I swear I even felt it move yesterday.'

Raphael and Annie shared a look across the top of Morgan's head. Annie was bewildered. What was going on here?

Raphael took Annie outside while their patient got dressed again.

'I think she has a ghost pregnancy,' he said.

'You mean a phantom pregnancy?' Annie was astonished. She had never come across one of those before, although she had read about them. Apparently it could happen when women so desperately wanted to be pregnant they managed to convince themselves that they were.

Raphael nodded. 'She must want a child very much.'

Annie could understand Morgan's feelings and her heart ached for her. She knew what it was like to yearn for a baby, to feel that something was missing from life. Although she had never imagined herself to be pregnant, she would have done anything to have a child.

Annie almost smiled at the irony of it. Robert hadn't loved her enough to want to adopt a child with her and now here was a man who was determined to be a father to her child, and she wasn't sure she wanted him around.

'I need to talk to Morgan,' she said.

'Would you prefer me to?' Raphael asked.

'No, she's my patient. It's my job,' Annie said heavily. 'But I wish I were about to tell her something different.'

Annie saw a distraught but resigned Morgan out a little later, and after finishing her paperwork for the day left for home herself. She was surprised to find Raphael waiting by the hospital exit. She nodded a goodnight in his direction, but he caught up with her and walked beside her.

'Are you okay?' he asked, searching her face. 'That must have been difficult for you.'

'I'm fine. It's all part of the job after all, isn't it? Most of the time our work has a happy outcome, but sometimes...' She shrugged. 'Things don't work out the way we want.'

'But it upset you. You tried not to show it, but I could see it on your face.'

There it was again. This man's uncanny

ability to perceive every emotion she felt. Even when she did her best to hide her feelings. Everyone thought nothing ruffled her, that she was able to keep herself emotionally detached, and she let them think that. Not least because it was the opposite of the truth. Her colleagues would be dismayed if they knew just how keenly she felt her patients' pain. Perhaps it was because she understood their longing for a child only too well.

'Yes, it did upset me. But I'll put it behind me. And move on.'

'Can you? Can you really put your feelings aside? Just like that?' He placed his hands on her shoulders, stopping her in her tracks before turning her around and looking into her eyes. She felt a dizzying sense of being caught up in his aura like a leaf in the wind. The rest of the world seemed to recede until it was just the two of them, in a bubble of their own. 'I need to know that you are okay,' he said roughly, breaking the spell and bringing her back to reality.

For a second Annie thought he was talking about her, but as his eyes dropped to her stomach she realised he was talking about her baby. Of course. Well, he had never pretended he was interested in her. As far as he was concerned, she was just a walking incubator for his child. She felt a flash of temper.

She sighed. 'Don't worry, Raphael. *I'm* still pregnant. And I will let you know if there is a problem.' However, seeing the look on his face, she took pity on him. It must be difficult to be a man sometimes. To feel excluded. But that wasn't her concern. He would just have to deal with it.

'The baby's fine, honestly,' she said. Then she couldn't help herself. 'I think I might have felt it move yesterday for the first time.'

His eyes glowed and he dropped a hand to her stomach. He left it there for a second. Once again Annie felt electrifying shocks shoot through her body and her knees turned to jelly.

She stepped away from him as if she'd been stung. 'Hey, you'd have to stand there for a long time if you're waiting to feel it move.' She looked around the car park. Although it was almost empty, there was always a chance somebody would see them and what they'd make of Dr Castillo with his hand on her belly was anyone's guess. One thing was for sure, though, she wasn't ready for anyone to know that he was the father of her child. Not yet, at any rate.

'You haven't told anyone, have you?' she said, suddenly horrified at the possibility that the identity of the father of her child was no longer a secret.

'No, just my mother. She is delighted that she is going to be a grandmother again. She remembers you well, the way you were with Maria, and thinks you will make a very good mother. She is looking forward to meeting her grandchild in a few months' time.'

Annie decided to let that pass. At least for the time being. She had no intention of letting her baby out of her sight and certainly not to Spain. Not without her at any rate. She had heard too many scary stories about kidnapped children and the way Raphael was about this baby, she'd put nothing past him.

She started back to her car. She didn't want to be rude but all she wanted to do was get home and gather her thoughts.

'Do you need a lift?' Annie asked. 'Or have you sorted yourself out with a car as well as a job?' She hadn't meant it to come out quite so waspishly, but the way this man was organising his life around her baby was unsettling her.

'Yes.' He waved in the direction of a sleek silver sports car. 'I drove it from Spain. And I have found a house in the village to live in, just ten minutes from your home.' He quirked an eyebrow at her, as if gauging her reaction to his news.

'So you're definitely staying, then?'

He looked surprised. '*Sí*. I told you I was. I accepted this job at the hospital. I cannot leave now, even if I wanted to.' He took a step towards Annie. 'You have to accept it. I am not going anywhere without my child.'

The next day was Saturday and Annie had been invited to a barbecue at Lucy and Ben's home. She didn't know Lucy, who was one of the doctors at the surgery and Nick's daughter, and who had gone on maternity leave before Annie had started at St Piran's, but she knew Ben, who was an A and E consultant at the hospital. She hadn't wanted to go, not sure she was ready to field questions about her own pregnancy, but Kate had pressed her.

'You should get to know more people in

Penhally, Annie. I know your friends and family are far away, and once you have the baby, you'll appreciate knowing more of the mothers. It's helpful to have someone to compare notes with.'

Annie waited until she knew the barbecue would be almost over. Sure enough, by the time she arrived, the guests with young children were already beginning to leave, although there was still loads of food. Tables had been laid out on the lawn, which overlooked the sea, and the scent of grilling sausages filled the air.

There were a few familiar faces as well as some that she didn't recognize, but there was one in particular that made her heart thump. She hadn't expected to see Raphael there.

As she greeted the other guests she watched Raphael from the corner of her eye. He looked completely at ease, as if he'd known everyone for years. It seemed as if he felt her eyes on him, because he turned and stared directly at her. Annie felt her breath catch in her throat. He really was the most beautiful man she had ever met, with his Latin colouring emphasised by his crisp white T-shirt and the faded jeans that clung to the contours of his thighs. Once again the memory of the night they had shared came rushing back. She remembered only too well the touch of his hands and mouth on her body, the way he had made her feel as if she were the only woman in the world, and the most beautiful woman he had ever held in his arms. And the intensity in his deep brown eyes told her he was remembering too. She felt a heat low in her body and she almost groaned aloud. Why did he have to come back into her life right now, when she thought she had everything all planned out?

Kate must have noticed her hovering on the fringe of the party. The older midwife came over and touched her briefly on the arm. 'Are you okay, Annie? You look as if you've seen a ghost. Do you want a drink of water or something?'

'No, I'm fine,' Annie said, summoning a smile, rubbing her lower back. A niggling ache had started that morning. She had put it down to the added weight of the baby putting a strain on her lower muscles, but an underlying anxiety that something was wrong wouldn't go away. For a split second she wondered whether to ask Kate's advice, but immediately dismissed the idea. She was probably just being over-anxious. Besides, she didn't want to draw attention to herself or ruin her friend's day off.

'I just feel a bit tired. You know how we are always telling our pregnant patients that it's normal to feel exhausted? It's quite different to experience it yourself.'

'You don't have to stay long,' Kate said. 'Lucy and Ben will understand.'

'Thanks, Kate. I'll probably just say hello to everyone, then make my excuses. But I'm dying to see little Josh again.'

She picked up an orange juice from a table and sipped the drink, happy to have something to distract her from Raphael. She glanced around.

Ben and Lucy were showing off their latest arrival, baby Josh, to a group of admirers. Apart from Chloe and her husband Oliver, a GP at Penhally Bay Surgery, there was Nick Tremayne with a blonde woman Annie hadn't seen before. Dragan Lovak, another of the partners, was there too, with his stunning wife, the village vet. Their young son sat at their feet, playing.

Annie went over to join them. It was the first time that she had been able to see a baby without feeling a wash of regret and she was happy to join in the crowd fussing over the cheerful, plump baby. Nevertheless, as she watched Oliver stand with his wife wrapped in the circle of his arms, she felt a sharp stab that she and her baby would never be part of a loving unit. She moved away, wanting to be alone with her thoughts.

How would it be to have Raphael around—a permanent part of her child's life, if not hers?

As if he could read her mind, Raphael excused himself from whatever conversation he'd been having with Ben and came towards her. For a moment she wanted to run away. Her heart was pattering away inside her chest and she was finding it difficult to breathe. Her symptoms only increased as he came to stand beside her.

'Dr Castillo,' Annie greeted him formally, aware of Kate's speculative gaze. 'I didn't expect to see you here.'

'Dr Carter—Ben—asked me. We met at the hospital. He thought it would be good for me to meet some of the locals. He knows I am far from home.'

'Everyone is very welcoming here. It's a small

community.' Annie let her eyes sweep the garden. Usually she avoided gatherings such as this one. Everyone always brought their children, and until now she had avoided occasions where she would see loving couples proudly showing off their offspring. But now everything was different. For the first time she could admire the babies without the tiniest bit of envy.

'Are you all right? You look pale,' Raphael asked, his eyes dropping to her belly. Once again Annie was reminded that, as far as he was concerned, she was little more than a human incubator for his unborn child. She felt a crippling stab of disappointment. But what else did she expect?

He was watching her, his brown eyes glinting, and she shivered. She wondered if he knew how much he affected her. He wasn't to know that the night they had spent together had been the most exhilarating night of her life, one she knew she would treasure for ever. He wasn't to know that she had been unable to get him out of her mind ever since. Thank God.

'I'm okay,' she said. 'If a little tired. I don't plan on staying long.'

Again there was a sharp look from eyes the colour of the mountains in the evening. His eyes raked her body.

He bent over and whispered in her ear. She could smell the tang of his aftershave and feel the heat of his breath on her neck. It took all her will-power not to shiver with delight. 'Pregnancy suits you,' he said softly. 'You are all curves and your face…' He hesitated as if searching for the right words. 'Your face is glowing. You don't look tired. You look beautiful.'

This time Annie couldn't prevent the blood staining her cheeks. There was something intimate in the way he spoke to her that made her feel as if they were the only two people in the world. 'If you want to leave,' he said, 'I will walk you home.'

'We don't want people to talk,' Annie managed through a dust-dry mouth. He had walked her home that night in Spain and look where that had led! Was he suggesting that they pick up where they had left off? Was he *flirting* with her? No, the idea was ridiculous.

Raphael looked around in surprise at the people gathered in the room. 'But they will have to know some time. Do you think you can keep us a secret for ever?'

'There is no "us",' she reminded him coolly.

'But there is. You, me and our child. I will be proud to be known as the father. And I am certain you are proud to be pregnant.'

'Of course I am, and everyone at the hospital knows about the baby already—I'm booked in at St Piran's after all. Kate, Chloe and Nick all know obviously, Kate's my midwife as well as my friend and Nick is my GP. But as for them knowing who the father is? Can't we keep that under wraps for the time being? Please?'

Raphael frowned. Then he smiled gently. 'If you wish. For the *time being*.' He echoed her words. 'It will give us a chance to get to know each other properly. Now, would you let me walk you home? It will give us the chance to talk.'

Suddenly Annie wanted nothing more than the comfort of her own house. Her mind was whirling, whether from Raphael's proximity or the promise in his words she couldn't be sure. As he had pointed out they did need to get to know each other—so that they could reach some sort of arrangement for their child. And she was curious to know more about this enigmatic man. For her baby's sake, of course.

'I just need to visit the bathroom first,' she said, trying to sound casual.

Since they'd been talking the dull ache she'd been experiencing earlier had grown in intensity. Her heart thudding, she told Raphael that she wouldn't be a minute, and hurried away.

When she made it to the toilet she was distraught to discover that she had begun to bleed. Not huge amounts admittedly, but enough to scare her witless. Was she having a miscarriage? She slid down onto the bathroom floor and hugged her knees to her chest, gasping as a wave of terror and shock raked her body. She *couldn't* lose this baby. Not now. Not when the dream she had longed for, had thought was out of her reach, had finally come true. But hadn't she, deep in her soul, known that it was too good to be true? That somehow it wasn't in her destiny to be a mother?

She didn't know how long she had sat there when she heard a soft tap at the door.

'Annie, are you all right?' Raphael's deep

tones penetrated the fog of grief and fear. She scrambled to her feet. He would know what to do. He would help her.

She opened the door and Raphael took one look at her face before gathering her into his arms.

'What is it? What is wrong?' he demanded. He held her at arm's length, forcing her to look at him. 'Is it the baby?'

Annie nodded, unable to speak. His face paled and she saw her anguish reflected in his eyes.

'What is happening?' he coaxed gently. 'Tell me exactly.'

Annie drew strength from him. 'I'm bleeding,' she said simply, and then in a rush the tears came and she was crying in his arms. 'My baby,' she gulped between the sobs that racked her body. 'I can't lose my baby.'

Raphael scooped her into his arms and carried her, still sobbing into his chest, past the startled glances of the other guests. Everyone stopped speaking for a moment and then Annie and Raphael were surrounded. But it was Kate who spoke first.

'What's wrong?' she asked quietly.

'She's bleeding. I am going to take her to St

Piran's.' Even in her distress, Annie could hear he was having difficulty keeping his voice even.

'I'll come with you,' Kate said. 'I'll drive while you take care of Annie.'

'I'll come too.' Annie recognized Chloe's anxious voice.

'We can manage, Chloe,' Kate said gently. 'Hopefully it's nothing serious. I'll call you later.'

And then Annie felt herself being lifted into the back of the car. Raphael covered her with his jacket before getting in beside her. He pulled her into his arms and stroked her head while her sobs turned to hiccups. Kate started the car and with a squeal of tyres headed towards St Piran's. They were the most dreadful minutes of Annie's life, but she was glad that Raphael was with her. He, more than anyone, would know what she was going through.

At the hospital, Raphael insisted on carrying her up to the maternity wing, Kate having to run alongside to keep up with him. Annie knew that come tomorrow, when all this was over, she would be mortified at all the attention. But right now she didn't care. If anyone could help her it was Raphael, and she trusted his medical skills absolutely.

He set her down on a couch in one of the examination rooms, calling for the ultrasound scanner in a voice that suggested that, if it wasn't brought to him this instant, there would be hell to pay. Fear closed Annie's throat and numbed her lips, but she answered Kate's questions as best she could. No, she hadn't bled before. She'd only had mild cramps tonight. Nothing until tonight. She had even felt the baby move earlier, but couldn't feel anything now.

Raphael, his eyes tight with concentration, was spreading cool gel on Annie's tummy. In any other circumstances she might have felt awkward as his hands lifted her dress, revealing her lacy underwear, but right now all she could think about was her baby.

Kate held her hand as Raphael scanned her abdomen, his attention fixed on the monitor. Suddenly his face creased into a smile and Annie felt the first small tug of hope since she had been to the bathroom.

'I can see the heartbeat,' Raphael said, relief in his voice. 'Look, Annie, there.' He turned the screen towards her and even through her swollen eyelids she could see the fluttering of a heartbeat. Her heart soared. She was still pregnant. For the time being, at any rate. She shook the thought away. She had to stay positive, for the baby's sake. There was no way she was going to give up on this baby, not until all hope was gone. And right now the baby was still there, inside her, needing her to be strong. She counted four limbs on the 3D image. Tiny legs folded and was it…? Yes, it was sucking its thumb. She felt a fresh wave of tears prick her eyes. But this time it was with relief and a wash of love. That was her baby, safe inside her womb.

It seemed as if Raphael was experiencing the same sea of emotions as he too stared at the tiny image. He muttered something in Spanish in a voice filled with awe. Kate was also smiling.

Through her relief, Annie was aware of Dr Gibson, her obstetrician, coming in to the room.

'The midwives told me our miracle mum was in,' she said. 'So I thought I'd pop in to see how you were.' She looked at Raphael, curiosity evident in her bright blue eyes. 'Although I can see Dr Castillo is already here.' She squinted at the monitor and nodded, looking satisfied.

'Baby looks fine, although I'm sure Dr Castillo has already told you that.'

'We should keep you in under observation, Annie. Just to be on the safe side,' Kate said.

'Will it make any difference if I stay?'

She saw Kate and Raphael exchange a look.

'No,' Raphael said gently. 'If you are going to miscarry, it will happen anyway.'

'Then I want to go home,' Annie said softly but firmly.

'I think you should stay,' Raphael responded. 'I will stay with you.'

Once again, Annie was aware of Dr Gibson's puzzled eyes on Raphael, before the older doctor looked at her.

'I know how much this pregnancy means to you, Annie. Particularly when you thought it could never happen. I don't think a night in hospital would do you any harm.' Dr Gibson turned to Raphael. 'I'm sure you'll be aware that Annie was thought to have ovarian failure.'

Raphael drew his brows together and Annie watched as realisation dawned that she had been telling him the truth. Emotions chased across his face. Delight followed by—could it be shame? Despite herself, she enjoyed watching him squirm.

Annie struggled into a sitting position and Kate came forward to help her.

'Look,' she said. 'We all know that it will make no difference whatsoever to the outcome if I stay in hospital. This pregnancy will either continue or...' Her voice broke. 'It won't. Staying here isn't going to change anything as you have just admitted. Am I right, Dr Gibson?'

'Yes. Bed rest won't make a difference. But you know that your medical history means you have to be extra-careful. So no vigorous exercise—and that includes penetrative sex. Just to be on the safe side.'

This time it was Annie's turn to squirm and she felt her face burn. Before she could help herself she slid a glance in Raphael's direction. Out of sight of Dr Gibson and Kate, he raised an eyebrow in her direction, a small smile tugging at the corner of his mouth. Her embarrassment deepened. Had the man no shame?

'I can't stay in hospital for the rest of my pregnancy,' Annie said, swinging her legs over the side of the bed. 'If I thought it would make the slightest difference, I would be happy to remain flat on my back and not move a muscle for the next few weeks or so. But it won't. So I'm going home where I feel more comfortable.'

'Okay, Annie,' Dr Gibson said, as her pager bleeped. 'You can go home if you wish, but remember what I said about taking it easy. I need to answer this, but come and see me at my clinic in about a week.'

'I'll stay at your house with you,' Kate offered after Dr Gibson had left the room. 'That way, you won't be alone if anything happens. We hope it won't, but we can't be sure. I can ask Rob if Jem could stay over at his house.'

But Raphael interrupted. 'No, I will. It is my responsibility.'

Kate narrowed her eyes and looked from Annie to Raphael. Annie could tell from the slow realisation dawning in her eyes that she was putting two and two together. What she made of Raphael being here in Penhally Bay was anyone's guess. But Annie knew that whatever her thoughts she would keep them to herself, and she was grateful for the older midwife's well-known discretion.

'I can stay on my own,' Annie protested. 'I have my phone. Kate only lives a short distance away. If I need her she can be with me in minutes.'

Irrationally Annie felt that if she stayed in the hospital, it would only make matters worse. At home she could pretend that everything was as it had been when she'd left the house earlier in the day.

'Either I stay with you at home, or you will stay here.' From the tone of Raphael's voice, Annie realised she wasn't going to win the battle. She didn't really have the strength for it. All she wanted now was to go home and climb into her own bed and sleep, comforted with the knowledge that her baby was okay.

'All right,' she agreed reluctantly. She would agree to anything as long as it got her out of the hospital. But she couldn't prevent a flicker of relief and happiness that Raphael would be coming home with her. If only for a night she could pretend it was for all the right reasons.

Kate dropped Annie and Raphael off at Annie's place with a final entreaty to Annie to call her any time, no matter what the hour, if she needed to. Once again, Raphael insisted on carrying her as if she was too fragile to stand on her own two feet, but for once she let him take care of her. She had looked after herself for so long, it felt strange but not unpleasant giving herself, even temporarily, into the care of someone else. In his arms she could believe that everything would turn out all right.

He laid her gently on her bed and insisted on removing her tights and her dress as if she were helpless. She felt every touch of his fingers burn into her skin. Then when she was left wearing only her bra and panties he looked down at her and she could hear his breath catch in his throat. But he shook his head and, muttering something in Spanish that sounded like a curse, he held the duvet up so she could crawl into bed. He surprised her even more by lying next to her, on top of the quilt, and pulling her into his arms so that her back rested against his chest. His hands were on her hair, soothing her, and she let herself drift away, secure in the knowledge that he was there if she needed him.

* * *

Raphael stroked Annie's dark brown hair, feeling the weight of it under his fingertips. He inhaled her perfume as her breathing deepened and became regular. He stole a glance at her sleeping face, the pale skin and tiny creases of worry at the corners of her eyes. He wondered if she had any idea how vulnerable she appeared despite that tough independent exterior. He was surprised by a rush of protectiveness she aroused in him. When he had come across her in the bathroom, one look at her had told him that she was almost destroyed at the thought of losing her baby. And he had been surprised at his own feelings, too. He wanted this baby, but the gut-wrenching sorrow he had felt when he had thought she had lost it had shaken him.

And then the realisation, back at the hospital, that she had been honest with him all along. He had misjudged her and felt acutely ashamed. Just because Ruth had lied to him, it didn't mean Annie was the same. He should have known she was telling the truth when she had been so adamant that she didn't want or need him in her life. He could only imagine what his reaction must have done to her. It would have taken courage to phone him, and then for him to doubt that the baby she was carrying was his. After everything she had gone through. Any other woman would have lashed out, but not Annie. She had done what she thought was right—for the baby.

There was no longer the slightest shred of doubt in his mind. She was carrying his baby. His child. And he hadn't been mistaken about Annie. She was the woman he had thought she was back in Spain. She had told him about the baby because she thought he had a right to know—not because she wanted anything from him. But was she as strong as she liked to make out? Somehow he doubted it. And as long as she was carrying his baby, he would stay and watch over them both—whatever she said.

CHAPTER SIX

WHEN Annie opened her eyes the next morning it was to the delicious aroma of fresh coffee. She stretched luxuriously beneath the sheets, unable to think at first who could be moving around in her cottage. But then the previous night's events came flooding back. She dropped her hands tentatively to her tummy, feeling the reassuring swell of her pregnancy, and then a tiny movement made her gasp. Her baby was still there, alive and kicking. She smiled to herself, feeling a bubble of happiness. One day at a time. She'd take one day at a time, just as she'd told so many of her patients.

Raphael appeared at the doorway, a tray balanced in his hands. Despite his rumpled appearance, Annie felt her breath catch in her throat. How could any man be so damned handsome? It just wasn't fair. As he walked towards her, she pulled the bedclothes up to her chin, suddenly self-conscious under his searching eyes. It was a bit late in the day, she thought ruefully, to be trying to hang onto her modesty. After all, this man had explored every inch of her already with his lips as well as his hands. She bit back a moan as a delicious heat flooded her body. She had to stop thinking about him in that way. No good could come of it. He was here because of his child. No other reason. And she'd do well to remember that.

'*Buenas días,*' he said evenly, but he couldn't quite hide the anxiety that darkened his eyes. If Annie had ever wondered how much he wanted this baby, any remaining doubts had disappeared when she'd sensed his anguish when he'd shared her fear that she might lose it. He propped the tray on her lap as she sat up.

'Morning,' she responded awkwardly. Then she added, 'I felt the baby kick just now.'

Knowing he would want to feel the reassuring movement as much as she did, she set the tray aside and took his hand, guiding it to her belly. As she felt his warm hand on her bare skin she felt goose-bumps prick her skin. Just then the baby moved and Annie was touched to see a look of relief and joy in his eyes. They smiled at each other and it was as if the air between them was alive. As if a cord bound them together. Or was it just their shared hope?

'My baby,' he said softly, before lowering his head and kissing her ever so gently on her small bump. Once more jolts of pleasure shot through her body. How was she going to cope having him around for the duration of her pregnancy if her body reacted like some wanton harpy every time he touched her?

As soon as he raised his head, she scrambled for the duvet again, snuggling under the protective folds. Not knowing what else to do to break the atmosphere that fizzled and sparked between them, she picked up her tray and almost laughed out loud. The coffee was fine, he had managed that, and the single rose clearly picked from outside her front door was a sweet touch, but the toast looked as if it had been dropped in water then wrung out and placed on her plate. What was he trying to do? Poison her?

He must have seen her look of incredulity as he looked hurt for a moment. '*Lo síento*—I am sorry about the toast,' he said. 'I didn't know what to do with it. I never eat my bread like that.'

'It's fine,' Annie said. 'I'm not particularly hungry, anyway. You needn't have bothered. I'm sure you'd rather be at home.'

'I am staying with you,' he said. 'I will go and change my clothes and then go to the shop and get us some proper breakfast. You stay where you are until I get back. Kate phoned to say she is coming to check on you, so she will be here with you while I am away.'

For a moment Annie was tempted to tell him to stop treating her as if she was a child, in fact, would everyone stop treating her like a child, but bit back the words. Right now she didn't have the energy nor the willpower to argue. As soon as he was gone she'd shower and dress. He would soon see that she wasn't the type of woman who he could order about. He might be used to getting his own way in Spain and at the hospital, but this was her house and she would do as she pleased.

'I didn't hear the phone,' she said.

'It has been ringing constantly, but I unplugged the extension in here so it wouldn't disturb you. So many people want to know that you are okay. So many people care about you.'

Annie sank back in the pillows. He was right, she knew that. But what about him? Did he care for her at all? And as for all these people who had phoned. What on earth had they thought when Raphael had answered? Hopefully, no more than one colleague looking out for another. Nevertheless, Annie knew that the jungle drums of Penhally Bay would be beating furiously. It was really only a matter of time before everyone guessed that Raphael was the father of her child. But she no longer cared who knew. The only thing that really mattered was the health of her baby.

Before she could ask him who exactly had phoned, there was a knock at the front door and she heard Kate's voice calling out. Raphael looked down at her, his eyes darkening. For a moment she imagined he looked reluctant to leave her. He leaned over towards her, and her breath caught in her throat. Was he going to kiss her? Her lips parted involuntarily but instead he brushed his fingertips against her cheek.

'I will see you soon,' he said, and headed for the door.

She could hear him and Kate talking in low voices, followed by the bang of the door. Moments later her friend popped her head around the door.

'Okay if I come in?' she asked.

'I don't seem to be able to stop anyone,' Annie grumbled before immediately feeling contrite. 'I'm sorry, Kate, please ignore me. I'm just feeling a little rattled, that's all. I can't help but feel that if everyone fusses around me, there must be something wrong.'

'Raphael said he felt the baby move. That's a good sign.'

'I know.' Annie sighed. 'But I can't help but worry.'

Kate's eyes were warm with sympathy. 'We're all going to do everything we can to get you through this,' she said gently. 'Everyone's rooting for you. I had to forbid them all from coming down here to see you in person. Although I suspect you'll want to see Chloe later?'

'Does she know? About Raphael?' Annie asked, easing herself out of bed and slipping her dressing gown on.

'I think most people, Chloe included, will have guessed who the father is,' Kate said. 'None of them are so stupid that they can't put your holiday in Spain together with the sudden arrival of Dr Castillo. According to Ben, Raphael used all his connections to get the job at St Piran's so he could be near you.' Kate smiled at Annie. 'Besides, people would have had to have been blind not to see how torn up he was last night. Most obstetricians don't go carrying patients around in their arms, even if they are the most caring of doctors.'

'He certainly cares about the baby,' Annie said softly. 'I've got the feeling he's going to be my personal physician for the rest of my pregnancy.'

'Would that be so bad?' Kate said. 'God knows, we can all do with support sometimes, no matter how strong we like to think we are inside.'

Annie thought Kate looked sad for a moment, but before she could say anything the smile was back.

'By the way, he said that your sister had phoned. Fiona, isn't it? He told her you'd call her back. I'll just make us some tea if you want to phone her now.'

Annie searched her house, eventually finding her phone in the kitchen, which incidentally looked as if a bomb had hit it. Whatever talents Raphael had, domesticity wasn't one of them. Leaving Kate in the kitchen, she wandered into her sitting room and dialled her sister's number.

After reassuring Fiona that, yes, she really was fine and, no, there was no need for her to leave her family and come to Penhally Bay and, yes, of course she would call if she changed her mind, Fiona asked about Raphael, agog to find he had come to work at St Piran's.

'I couldn't believe it when he answered the phone,' she said. 'Then he told me what had happened, but that you and the baby were fine. So, Annie, what's the deal? Why didn't you tell me he had followed you? Are you two going to be together? I'm so excited for you.'

'I can't talk now,' Annie told her sister. 'I've visitors. I'll call later. But don't get too excited about Raphael being here. It's not what you think. And, Fi, don't tell Mum and Dad about last night. They'll only worry and insist on coming home early. And there's really nothing anyone can do.'

Annie hung up when she heard Chloe talking to Kate. She went into her kitchen and the young midwife handed her a cup of tea.

'How are you doing?' she asked. 'Kate says everything has settled down. She was good enough to phone me after she dropped you off, otherwise I wouldn't have slept a wink, worrying.'

Annie was grateful for the genuine concern in Chloe's eyes, but hurried to reassure her.

'And I understand our new doctor refused to leave your side.'

Annie didn't miss the teasing look she sent her way. She felt herself blush furiously.

'Does everyone know?' she asked.

'What about?' Chloe asked innocently.

Annie could feel her face get warmer. 'Do people know who the father is?'

'There is gossip. You must know there was bound to be, but most of it is just kindly interest. However, I'm afraid the way that our Dr Castillo carried you off and refused to budge from your side was a bit of a give-away.'

'I suppose it was inevitable that people put two and two together,' Annie said.

'Especially those who knew about your

holiday in Spain. No one knew there was a vacancy at the hospital when, lo and behold, Dr Castillo turns up. Rumour has it that he called in every favour he was owed, to get the job. So, yes, I'm afraid the cat is well and truly out the bag. Do you mind very much?'

'No, I guess not,' Annie said quietly. 'People were bound to find out sooner or later. He's an experienced doctor, too. Anyway, St Piran's is lucky to have someone with his experience.'

'And what about you, Annie? How do you feel about him being here?' Chloe asked quietly.

How could she answer Chloe's question when she didn't know the answer herself? Annie knew she felt the same way about him as she had from the moment they had met. And that wasn't good. He would never feel the same way about her. And what if he carried out his threat to claim his rights as a father and demanded shared access? She didn't want her child to spend half its life away from her in Spain.

'I'm not sure. I don't really know that much about him,' Annie said evasively. 'I know he comes from a big extended Spanish family but that's about it.' She felt herself grow warm under their scrutiny. She wished she could at least say that they had been together the whole two weeks while she'd been in Spain, that their child had been conceived after spending time together, instead of it being obvious that she had spent very little time in the man's company before jumping into bed with him. She just knew she couldn't explain the instant, overwhelming attraction she had felt for Raphael.

'But anyway,' she continued, 'that is neither here nor there. As far as he is concerned, the baby is his and he is determined to stick around. Or so he says.' Annie hesitated then decided to confide in Chloe and Kate, knowing that neither woman would ever break a confidence.

'He tells me he intends to apply for legal access. What if he takes my baby to Spain for a visit and never brings him back?'

Two pairs of eyes studied her sympathetically.

'I don't think he could do that,' Kate said reassuringly. 'Anyway, the mother usually wins—what do they call it now—rights of residence.'

'But these days fathers have equal rights, don't they?' Annie tried to keep the panic out of her voice.

'Why don't you speak to him about it, Annie?' Kate suggested. 'It could be that you're worried about nothing. Maybe he'll put your mind at rest.'

Kate was right, of course. Annie needed to face up to the situation like the grown woman she was. But she couldn't help wondering whether she had done the right thing in letting Raphael know he was the father of her child. How much less complicated it would have been had she said nothing at all.

Kate and Chloe left shortly after Raphael arrived back. He had showered, and dressed in a thin cashmere pullover with a pair of jeans, looking, Annie thought, sexy as hell. Every time Annie saw him she remembered how he had made her feel that first night. How the atmosphere between them had seemed charged with electricity. But so far he was still an enigma to her. One thing was for sure, though, if the baby inherited its father's dark good looks it would be beautiful.

'What are you doing out of bed?' he growled at her. 'I thought we agreed you were going to stay in bed for the weekend and let me look after you?'

Once again Annie felt exasperated. While she welcomed his support, there was no way he was going to tell her how to live her life. Didn't he know that she would do whatever she could to protect the life growing inside her?

'Actually, no,' Annie said firmly. 'I agreed to nothing. As I said before, you and I both know that me staying in bed won't change a thing.'

'I had no idea you were so stubborn,' he said, his mouth twitching. 'But you will find out I am stubborn, too.' Before she had a chance to protest he had crossed the room and scooped her up in his arms. Annie had no choice but to wrap her arms around his neck and cling on for dear life while he marched into the bedroom and laid her, as if she could break in two, gently on the bed.

As he looked down at her, his eyes glowing, Annie felt her breath catch in her throat. For a second the world stood still and her treacherous body yearned to feel his hands on her once more. He bent over her and brushed a stray curl away from her face with a gentle finger. *'Dios,'* he said hoarsely, 'why do you have to look at me like that?' And then, almost as if he couldn't bear the sight of her, he straightened and moved to the other side of the room, apparently determined to put as much space as possible between them.

'I have brought supplies from the shop as well as newspapers and magazines. I had no idea what you like, so I bought the lot. I will bring them to you.'

By this time Annie had had enough. Raphael had to understand that she didn't need him fussing over her like a mother hen. If he wanted to stick around she had to make him realise that she needed to do things her way. For all she knew, he could disappear back to Spain at any time, leaving her to get on with it on her own, and the last thing she wanted was to become reliant on somebody who might not stick around. She knew he was enamoured with the idea of becoming a father, any idiot could see that, but what about when the harsh realities of being a parent struck home? Would he be so keen then? She had fought so hard for her independence, she was damned if she was going to give it all up now. Just because it suited him.

'I'm going for a shower,' she said. 'Then I'm going to get dressed. You,' she said crossly, 'can do what you like.' She felt a moment of pleasure as she saw the look of surprise on his face. Then she hopped out of bed and, wrapping the sheet around her as well as much of her dignity as she could salvage, she stalked off to the bathroom without a backward glance.

By the time Annie came out of her deliberately long shower, Raphael was nowhere to be seen. She ignored the flash of disappointment and, selecting a dress that was loose around the waist, finished dressing. She dried her hair, taking her time over the ritual until her brown hair was tamed into a neat bob. Now she felt almost human again and ready to face the world. There was no more spotting and no cramping. Everything seemed to have settled down.

'Hey, you,' she said softly laying a hand on her belly, 'you just keep fighting in there. You have a mummy who wants you more than anything in the world and who already loves you more than she can say.' As if in response to her encouragement the baby moved and Annie felt a surge of relief. It was a fighter, this little one. It was a miracle it was here in the first place.

She padded through to her sitting room. As he'd promised, Raphael had left enough magazines and newspapers to keep her occupied for the rest of her pregnancy, never mind the weekend. She frowned in confusion as she leafed through the pile. He had even included a copy of *Biker's Weekly*! She smiled, imagining him in the newsagent's, grabbing the first magazines that came to hand, unsure what she liked to read and in too much of a hurry to get back to check up on her to think about it. Her smile faded as another thought hit her—or did it show how little they knew of about one another? And yet they were going to parent the same child. She picked up a well-known travel magazine with a four-page spread on the part of Spain he came from. Now, was that deliberate? she wondered. Was he determined to persuade her to bring their baby to Spain? She couldn't make up her mind whether to be amused or angry. In fact, everything about Raphael confused her. She had been content on her own, and as soon as she'd known she was going to have a baby, her life had been complete. But now that he was back in her life again, all testosterone, making her go weak at the knees every time she saw him, he had gone and upset everything all over again. In many ways it would have been better if he had stayed out of her life.

Looking out the window, she saw that the sun was shining. It was a perfect early summer day and Annie felt restless. Maybe she should practise some yoga? That always calmed her and no one could say it counted as vigorous exercise. She felt her cheeks grow warm as she remembered what else Dr Gibson had said. No penetrative sex. As if! There was no worry on that score! It was clear that any desire Raphael might have had for her had long since vanished. Although when he had raised an eyebrow at her, back there in the hospital room, she had seen from his eyes that he had been thinking of the night they'd conceived the baby. She crossed over to the window and opened it, letting the gentle breeze cool her cheeks. It was a lovely day. Perhaps she would go for the walk she had threatened, but she didn't feel confident enough to go on her own. Whatever she had told Raphael, she was still scared—no, terrified—that she could yet lose her baby.

CHAPTER SEVEN

ANNIE was beginning to feel hungry when there was a tap on the door. She opened it to find Raphael standing there, holding another bunch of flowers. For a moment she was taken aback. It was almost as if he was wooing her. Despite everything she had told herself, she couldn't help a tiny spurt of pleasure at the gesture. But she needed to remember that this man would do anything to make sure he was kept in her baby's life. She mustn't let his little-boy grin get to her.

In addition to the flowers, Raphael was laden with cardboard boxes that smelled delicious.

'I had a look in your fridge earlier,' he said, 'but there was nothing. Don't you know you have to eat? To stay strong?'

'I know. For the baby,' Annie retorted.

'Isn't that what we both want?' He looked puzzled.

'Yes. Of course.' Annie was suddenly aghast. What was she thinking? That she wanted him to see her as more than the mother of his child? That she wanted him to see her as a woman? But she didn't. She would never have a relationship with a man who threatened her with lawyers. But he still hadn't actually told her what he was planning to do when the baby arrived. She should take Kate's advice and talk to him about it.

'We need to talk,' he said, as if he'd read her mind. 'But first we need to eat. I for one cannot think on an empty stomach. I was going to cook for us, but I don't know what you like—except seafood. But best not to chance that while you're pregnant. So I got a selection of other things I thought you might like from the restaurant on the main street.'

He emptied the contents of the boxes onto plates he had fetched from the kitchen.

'Remembering the way you cook,' Annie said, smiling, 'I think you did the right thing.'

Raphael pretended to look hurt for a moment. Then he grinned and Annie's heart somersaulted.

'I thought about going for a walk later,' Annie said. 'I hate being cooped up inside. Especially when the weather is so perfect.'

Raphael's smile was replaced by a frown. 'I thought we agreed you were going to rest—at least for a day or two.'

Annie replied, not even attempting to hide her frustration, 'Dr Gibson said no vigorous exercise. I hardly think a stroll falls into that category.' She blushed, remembering what else Dr Gibson had said. 'You can hardly stand guard over me for the rest of the pregnancy, Raphael!'

Raphael put his fork down and, reaching across the table, took Annie's hand.

'Cariño,' he said softly. 'If I thought standing guard over you would help, I wouldn't leave your side, but as you are determined to go for a walk, there is nothing for it except that I go too!'

Before Annie could protest, he dropped her hand and touched her lips with his finger. Annie swallowed a moan as her body thrilled to his touch.

'No more arguments,' he continued, tracing the line of her lips. 'You will find I can be as stubborn as you. Now—' he looked at her with mock severity, thankfully unaware of Annie's furiously beating heart '—let's finish eating. Or make no mistake—you won't be leaving this house.'

After they had eaten, they followed the road down towards the shore. The early evening was warm and the scent of flowers and sea filled the air. Annie loved this time of year in Penhally Bay. Soon she would need to make a start on converting the spare room into a nursery and had already decided she would paint it butter-cup yellow.

They followed the road until they came to the lighthouse.

They stood in companionable silence for a moment, watching as the sun turned the sky to strips of red, gold and lilac. Eventually Raphael turned molten brown eyes on her.

'I owe you an apology and an explanation,' he said. 'I should never have doubted you and I cannot have you worrying about me taking the baby from you. You must understand I would never do that. It is not easy for me to tell you why I went to a lawyer, but I feel I must. Can I ask you not to tell anyone else—do I have your word?'

'I can keep a confidence,' Annie said.

Raphael took a deep breath before speaking. 'I was married. Until last year.'

Annie felt her heart thump. Was he going to tell her he was still in love with his wife?

'My wife and I had a child. Sebastian. He is three now.' Raphael smiled grimly before continuing, 'I love that little boy. He is my life.'

Annie drew in a breath. The pain in his voice was evident. She hadn't known he had a child. Where was he? And what was Raphael doing so far away from his him? If he loved him, and it was evident he did, how could he bear to be away from him?

She waited quietly for him to continue. It was obvious he was having difficulty keeping his emotions in check. His eyes were dark and Annie had to sit on her hands to prevent herself leaning towards him and brushing the stray lock of hair from his eyes.

'My wife left me,' he said baldly. 'And she took my son with her. Only it turned out that Sebastian wasn't my son after all. He belonged to the man she ran off with.'

Annie was appalled. But in that instant she knew more about Raphael than she had thought possible. His hurt was written all over his face.

'I'm sorry,' she said. 'That must have been hard.' She longed to reach out and comfort him, but something in the way he held himself, in his forbidding expression, warned her that he wouldn't welcome her touch.

'She wouldn't let me see him. So I went to the court and asked for access. But it was denied. They said that I wasn't the biological father, so I had no rights.'

The bitterness and pain in his voice shook Annie. No wonder he was so determined to have some legal rights to their child.

'It didn't matter that I was the only father he had ever known, that he loved me and I loved him. None of that counted when it came to access. She took him away to another part of Spain. I don't know how he is, if he is missing me. I know nothing about my child's life. And he *is* my child. Even if I am not the biological father.'

'I'm so sorry, Raphael. I can only imagine what that must be like for you. Not to be able to see him. Not to have any contact whatsoever.'

He stood up and turned away as if he couldn't bear to look at her. 'I don't want your sympathy,' he said roughly. 'I just need to be certain that the same thing won't happen again.'

Annie's blood chilled. But it must be difficult for this proud man to admit that he had been deceived.

'Did you love her very much?' she said quietly. 'Your ex-wife?'

'Ruth? I told myself I loved her. When she told me she was pregnant with my child, I asked her to marry me. I thought we could make it work. For the sake of the child. But we were never really happy, and eventually she met with the real father again.' His voice was bitter with the memory. 'She started seeing him again while she was still married to me. I was such a fool.'

This time Annie couldn't help herself. She got up and went to stand beside him, touching his arm. He flinched almost as if she had burnt him.

'And Sebastian? What about him?'

His voice was raw when he spoke. 'Whatever she says, he *is* my son. I was the one who looked after him in the night when he couldn't sleep. The one who kissed his knee when he scraped it. Whatever the court says, he is still my son.'

'Do you see him at all?'

'No. That is why I am speaking to the lawyers

about this baby.' He smiled grimly, still looking into the distance. 'I can't lose this child too. You must see that.'

Annie *could* see it. Just by looking at him she could tell how badly he had been hurt. More than hurt, betrayed. It was the sadness she had seen inside him the night they had first met. And it was still there. But that didn't mean she could risk losing control over her child's future to appease a hurt Raphael had experienced at the hands of another woman. No matter how sympathetic she felt.

'I wouldn't stop you seeing your child. Not unless I thought it was harmful in some way. Can't you trust me to do the right thing? After all, I needn't have told you I was pregnant.'

'I know. I misjudged you. And for that I am sorry. Can we start over again? Please?' He smiled his killer smile which never failed to make Annie go weak at the knees.

She felt a shiver of excitement, and her heart beat faster. Did he mean start over from where they had left off in Spain? Did he still feel that same connection she did?

'Can we be friends for the sake of our child?

Work something out between us?' Raphael continued.

Annie's heart plummeted. Of course, she should have known. All he was interested in was the child. But he had a point—no matter how disappointed she felt that he didn't want anything more than friendship from her, they needed to reach an agreement about what was going to happen once the baby was born.

'You can come and see him any time you like,' Annie said through stiff lips.

Raphael drew his brows together. 'But I would also want him to come to Spain. He must get to know his family, what it is to be Spanish. I would want him to visit often.'

Instinctively, Annie placed her hands protectively on her belly. Could she trust him? This man she barely knew, yet was the father of her child? How was she going to bring herself to let this precious little one out her sight for a second, never mind to another country.

'Don't you trust me?' he asked softly, as if he had guessed what she was thinking. 'What can I do to make you believe me that I only want to do what is right for my child?'

Raphael raised a finger to her cheek, tracing a line down to her jaw. She couldn't have felt his touch more keenly if he was drawing a knife across her skin. 'What are you thinking? Please—tell me, *cariño*.'

This time it was Annie who drew away. She wrapped her arms around her body.

'A year ago, I was going to get married, to Robert. We had known each other almost all our lives and planned to have a large family,' Annie said slowly after a few moments. 'But my periods had been irregular for years and somebody at the clinic I worked in, back in Edinburgh, suggested I have a fertility test.' She looked into the distance, remembering. 'I took it more out of curiosity than anything else. It never really occurred to me that there could be a problem.'

'What was this test?' Raphael asked.

'It's called an AMH. It's fairly new but deemed to be very reliable.'

Raphael nodded. 'I have read about it in the medical journals.'

'Apparently my ovarian reserve was so low that even IVF would be out of the question.'

Raphael looked at her steadily.

'Go on,' he said.

'It hadn't even crossed my mind that there wasn't plenty of time to think about having a child. You don't think when you're twenty-seven that it's already too late do you? At least, I didn't.' She remembered only too well her feeling of shock and disbelief. 'When I told Robert he was dismayed. And once he realised that even IVF was out of the question, he began to change. I told him that we could always adopt, but he said that he could never bring up another man's child. After that we drifted apart. There was no more talk of weddings. I realised he couldn't love me the way I thought he did, so I called the whole thing off. I think he was relieved. That's when I decided to come to Penhally Bay. To start afresh. But the pain follows you, you know. It's ironic, being a midwife. Every day you're confronted with what you can't have. Don't get me wrong, I love my job and I love bringing happiness to all these couples, but it used to hurt.'

'He couldn't be much of a man, this Robert,' Raphael said, frowning.

'I can't blame him. He wanted something I couldn't give him. It was unfair to expect him to give up the chance of a family for me.'

'If you were my woman, I wouldn't have let you go. You should be with someone because you have to be. Not because you want children.' His eyes were warm with sympathy. 'But now I understand. Our baby will be very special for you. But for me, also.'

Annie nodded, relieved that he seemed to understand. 'Raphael, this baby is like a miracle to me. I can't believe how lucky I am. It's unlikely, though, that I will ever fall pregnant again. This is my one chance to have a child.' Annie struggled to keep her voice even. She knew there was no way that she could convey properly how devastated she had been when she had thought having a child of her own was an impossibility. And anyway, did she want to reveal anything more of herself to this man? She had already shown him too much of her soul. He was the father of her child, that was all, and she'd do well to remember that. Even if it almost broke her heart.

CHAPTER EIGHT

A FEW weeks later, Annie was back at work, feeling much more rested. She was surprised to find Claire and Roy waiting to see her. Claire wasn't due to come in for another couple of weeks and Annie was immediately concerned to see her back so soon. She was even more worried when she saw the look of anxiety on the couple's faces.

'What is it Claire?' Annie asked gently. 'What's bothering you? Is it the babies?'

'I've had a little spotting,' Claire said anxiously. 'I know it can happen sometimes, but—'

'We just wanted to make sure everything was all right,' Roy finished for her.

Annie's heart went out to the couple. She knew they'd be terrified. Claire had seemed so fragile the last time Annie had seen her that she was worried that if she lost the babies she would sink so far into depression that she might not come out the other side. Claire was already in her late thirties and the chance of another pregnancy was diminishing with every passing year.

'I'm going to page Dr Castillo. His special interest is high-risk pregnancies and I'm sure he'll want to scan you, Claire, to see what exactly is going on. I'll ask him to come as soon as he's free. In the meantime, could you try and drink as much as possible so your bladder is nice and full for the scan?'

Claire's eyes filled with tears and she reached for Roy's hand. 'I'm so scared, Annie,' she said shakily. 'I don't know if it's better not knowing, if you see what I mean? As long as I don't know I—we—still have hope.'

Annie stood up and went over to Claire and wrapped her in her arms. 'You're way ahead of yourself. I know how scary all this can be. Believe me. Let's just take one step at a time, okay?'

When Claire nodded, Annie picked up the phone and asked switchboard to page Dr Castillo. While she waited for him to answer she filled a glass of water from the jug on her desk and handed it to Claire.

'Dr Castillo.' Annie heard his deep voice on the other end of the phone. 'You were paging me?'

'Dr Castillo,' she said formally. 'It's Annie. I have someone I'd like you to scan. Could you come down to the antenatal clinic?'

'I'm due in theatre in fifteen minutes. Can it wait until later?'

Annie looked over at Claire, who was drinking the water as if her life depended on it. 'No,' she said, 'it can't.'

'Are you all right?' Immediately the concern was back in his voice.

'Of course,' Annie said. 'It's a couple with a twin IVF pregnancy. She's had some bleeding and is feeling anxious.'

'I'll be right there,' Raphael said, and disconnected.

Annie only had enough time to prepare Claire for the scan before Raphael arrived. He was wearing his theatre scrubs, which framed his muscular body perfectly. Once more, despite herself, Annie felt a thrill when he came into the room. Must be the pregnancy sending her hormones into overdrive, she told herself.

Raphael introduced himself to the worried

couple and his easy and relaxed manner soon put them at ease.

While he set up the scanning machine Annie gave him an overview of Claire's history to date. 'This is their third attempt at IVF. Neither of the first two goes resulted in a pregnancy, but this time both the embryos put back implanted successfully. Claire had a scan around seven weeks and two heartbeats were clearly visible at that stage. She's been well up until now, but had some spotting last night. They thought it best to have it checked out.'

Raphael caught Annie's eye. It was obvious from the sympathetic look in his eyes that he knew how close to the bone seeing Claire was for her.

'How many weeks into the pregnancy are you?' he asked Claire, bringing her into the conversation.

'Twenty-four,' Claire replied.

Roy held his wife's hand as Annie covered her stomach in ultrasound gel. They all watched the screen as Raphael scanned. As the image came up on the monitor, Annie could immediately make out two heartbeats. She felt a surge of relief, but almost as quickly it was replaced with concern. While two babies were clearly visible, neither of the babies were the size they should be for the dates. To make matters worse, one was significantly bigger than the other. As Raphael turned to look at her, she could see he shared her concern.

'I have some good news for you and some not-so-good news,' he said gently. 'As you can see from the monitor—' he indicated the two beating hearts with his finger '—there are two heart beats—there and there.' Claire and Roy craned their heads to see what he was showing them. 'The problem, however, is that one baby—' he pointed to one of the tiny forms '—is significantly smaller than the other. This suggests that the bigger baby is taking more than its fair share of the nutrients from the placenta, meaning that the smaller baby is struggling to get enough to grow.'

'What does it mean?' Roy asked.

'It means,' Raphael said, 'that both your babies are still alive. That's the good news. However, we will have to monitor both of them carefully over the next couple of weeks. If it looks like the second baby isn't getting enough nutrients, we will have to think about what to do.'

'What might those options be?' Although Roy's voice was calm, Annie knew he was only keeping it together for Claire's sake.

Raphael looked at him sympathetically.

'It's too soon to know. As I said, we will monitor your babies very closely over the next couple of weeks. Keep an eye on their growth.'

'And if the second baby doesn't grow? What then?' Roy insisted. 'Look—' he turned to his wife and gripped her hand tightly '—we'd both prefer to know, so please tell us. What is the worst that can happen?'

'We might have to deliver the twins much earlier than we would like. I know this a lot for you to take in, and I believe it is important for patients to have all the facts so they can be fully involved in the decision making process, but I am not ready to make that decision yet. As I say, we should wait and see how they get on.'

Claire turned terrified eyes to Annie.

'I don't understand,' she said. 'Annie, is there a chance my babies could die?'

Annie put her arms around the distraught woman's shoulders. 'There's nothing to suggest that right now, Claire. I know all this is difficult for you to take in. But you are lucky to have Dr Castillo to look after you. He is one of the leading experts in his field. We have to trust him.'

Raphael looked at Annie, seeming surprised at her warm endorsement, but then he turned to the couple.

'I want you to go home and try not to worry, even though I know that will be difficult. I will scan you again in two weeks' time. We will have another look at your babies then, and think about what to do. In the meantime, all we can do is wait.'

And pray, Annie thought. Pray that this couple weren't going to have their dreams dashed. But Raphael was right, there was nothing more that could be done right now.

She made another appointment for Claire and Roy to come back to see her and Raphael before seeing them out of the department. When she returned to the room, Raphael was still there, writing in Claire's notes.

'What do you really think?' she asked him.

He looked up at her, surprised. 'Exactly what I told them. We'll know more in a couple of weeks. In the meantime, all we can do is wait.'

'Couldn't we have waited until the next scan? Now they'll have days of worry to live through when it might not be necessary.'

Raphael narrowed his eyes at her. 'I believe that parents have the right to know all the details. The days when doctors decided to hold back information from their patients for their own good are gone. No?'

'But if it means putting them through unnecessary worry? Can't you see how terrified they are?'

Raphael leaned back in his chair and looked at Annie thoughtfully. 'Tell me,' he said softly, 'if you were in her shoes, would you want to know the truth?'

Annie knew she was being unreasonable but she couldn't help herself. Having experienced the terror of thinking she was about to lose a desperately wanted child, she knew exactly what Claire was going through. Raphael leaned across the desk and touched her arm gently.

'They asked me for the truth, Annie. I couldn't do anything else but tell them. Can't you see that?' He dropped his hand. 'Maybe you are getting too close to your patients. We need to keep some professional distance, otherwise we can't help them.'

Suddenly all the anger went out of Annie. Raphael was right. Roy had asked and he had deserved an honest answer. And Raphael was right too about her letting her personal feelings get in the way. If she were to help the couple, she needed to keep her perspective.

Later that day Annie saw Mrs Duncan, a smiling mother of four young children.

'Nurse Kate sent me here for a scan,' she said, settling herself into the chair. 'I'm pregnant again. Number five! I know it's a bit unexpected—for me, too—but the more the merrier, I say.'

Annie looked at Mrs Duncan's notes. Her last pregnancies had been straightforward and Kate had looked after her at the surgery. The first two had been born at St Piran's and the last two at home, with Kate in attendance.

Instantly she was concerned. Mrs Duncan had been in her mid-thirties when her first child had been conceived and almost forty when her youngest, now four and a half, had been born. At almost forty-five Annie knew that the chances of the baby having some sort of abnormality were significantly raised. No doubt the same thought had occurred to Kate and that was why she had sent the woman to Annie's clinic for a nuchal scan. But it seemed as if the reason for the scan hadn't really sunk in with the happy woman in front of her.

'It's not the best timing,' Mrs Duncan continued. 'Not with the six of us still living in the caravan while our house is being rebuilt. Although we should be back in our own house by the time this one is ready to be born.'

Annie shivered as she remembered the storm that had devasted a large part of Penhally Bay months earlier. The buildings that had been damaged were almost repaired but two people had lost their lives and no amount of rebuilding would ever completely undo the trauma of that day in people's minds. She couldn't help but admire her patient's cheerfulness in the face of what must be very demanding circumstances.

'I'm sure Kate told you why she was sending you here for a scan, Mrs Duncan?' Annie asked. Of course, the senior midwife at Penhally Bay Surgery would have explained it all to her patient, but from Mrs Duncan's cheerful attitude, Annie sensed that she didn't seem to realise that she had a significantly higher chance of a chromosomal abnormality in this pregnancy.

'Oh, please call me Mary,' the older woman said. 'And, yes, Nurse Kate said that everyone was offered a scan when they were twelve weeks now. So that's why I'm here. I'll have my scan and then if you could give me the picture, I'll be on my way.'

Annie suppressed a smile, before inviting Mary up onto the couch. News of the brand-new scanner they had at St Piran's had spread quickly. The 3D images were clear enough to see even minute details and patients loved taking home photographs of the images. But almost as soon as she started to scan Mary, she could see that her instincts had been right. The nuchal fold, indicating an increased chance of Down's syndrome, was obviously thicker than normal. Her heart sank.

Mary quickly sensed that something was wrong. She squinted at the screen and then turned to look at Annie.

'What is it?' she asked. 'There's something wrong, isn't there? I can tell from the look on your face.'

'I'll need to do a blood test to confirm it, but I have to tell you that there are signs that your baby has a higher risk of Down's syndrome. If the blood test comes back positive, you may wish to think about amniocentesis.'

'What's that when it's at home? Anyway, I thought that was why I was having this scan.'

'This scan and blood test only tells us whether you have an increased risk. We need to do another test to confirm the result.'

'I think Nurse Kate suggested I might want that test with my last one,' Mary said slowly, 'but I decided against it. And my baby was fine. All my babies have been fine. So surely I don't need to worry about that?'

'The older a mother gets, the greater the risk of a Down's syndrome baby. The test does carry a small risk of miscarriage with it. You'll need to weigh up the pros and cons. You don't have to have the test, but you should consider it.'

'If you think I should then I will.' Mrs Duncan replied cautiously. 'I'm not sure I could cope with a disabled child, not when I have four of them and we're all crammed into the tiny caravan up in the park.'

Annie could see how deflated she was. Mrs Duncan had come in full of hope and excitement and all Annie had done was burst her bubble. But, as Raphael had just pointed out, she wouldn't be doing her job if she didn't give her patients all the facts and let them make up their own minds.

'I think you should have a word with the doctor before you go. If you can wait a few minutes, I'll give him a shout.'

Mary nodded. Annie left the room and went in search of Raphael. Fortunately she caught him just as he was seeing a patient out.

'I have someone in with me I'd like you to see,' Annie said. 'When I did her booking scan I could see a larger than normal nuchal fold. I'm not sure whether to arrange for her to come back for amniocentesis in three weeks or whether we should be doing a CVS today. I suspect that depends on what you think and whether you have time.'

Raphael took Mary's notes and the picture of the scan Annie had taken. 'You're absolutely right about the nuchal fold,' he agreed. 'The hospital is lucky to have a midwife who can scan. It is much more efficient this way.' He held his hands up and grinned as Annie started to speak. 'I know you are highly trained. I recognise that. Shall we see Mrs Duncan?'

Mrs Duncan had finished dressing by the time Annie and Raphael returned. Although pale, she seemed composed.

'I gather Annie here has explained things to you?' Raphael said gently. 'I realise it's probably a bit of a shock, but we are going to do everything we can to help you make the right decision for you. Okay?'

Mary nodded.

'There are three options here. One—we do nothing. Two—we bring you back for an amniocentesis. That's where we take a sample of the fluid surrounding the baby in the womb. We can only do that when you are a little further on.' He glanced at the notes. 'In about three weeks' time. The third option is that we can do a test today where we take a sample of the placenta. I have to warn you that both the tests carry a risk of miscarriage. So we have to weigh up whether the risks outweigh the benefits. Do you understand all this?'

'I think so.' Mary turned frightened eyes on Annie. 'What do you think?'

'I think you should go home and speak to your husband about it before you decide anything.'

'But Bill's away fishing. He won't be back for another three days—at least.'

'Another few days won't make much difference either way, and it's something you should speak to him about. We can, of course, do the CVS today, but I really feel you should take some time to think about it. I can also ask Kate to pop around and see you, if that helps. I know you saw her through your last pregnancies and sometimes it helps to talk things over with someone else before coming to a decision.'

'Doctor?' Mary turned to Raphael.

'I think it's good advice. Some women decide not to have the test at all, but I'm afraid it has to be your decision. Whatever you decide, whenever you decide, we will be here to help.'

'I think I will wait, then. Can I let you know when I make up my mind?'

'Of course, Mary. The important thing is not to leave it beyond sixteen weeks. Having a termination after that can be very hard, if that's what you eventually decide to do.'

'And I think it would be useful if I gave you

some stuff explaining about Down's syndrome to take away with you,' Annie interrupted. 'Many women find that these children can bring a lot of joy to the family. It may not be right for you, but think about it.'

As soon as Annie had seen Mary out, armed with all the literature she could find for her, as well as a few useful Internet sites that she might want to look at, Annie went in search of Raphael. She found him talking to one of the junior doctors at the reception desk. As soon as he noticed her he came towards her and, taking her by the arm, took her to one side out of the hearing of his colleague.

'What is it?' he said. 'You are pale. There's nothing wrong with the baby, is there?'

'No, everything's fine. It's just…' She tailed off, uncertain why she had sought Raphael out but knowing she needed to speak to him. Maybe it was the threatened miscarriage and the knowledge that she had an increased chance of going into early labour. She was so scared for her baby.

'Seeing these patients makes you worry about your own pregnancy. Is that it?' His warm brown eyes searched hers. He raised a hand to her face and brushed her cheek with a fingertip. 'It must be hard for you.'

'I'm just so frightened,' she admitted. 'I know the chances of me going into early labour are increased and, well, we both know what that could mean.'

Raphael put his hands on her shoulders, and ignoring the presence of his junior, pulled her close.

'I know you are frightened. Try not to be. I am here with you.'

Annie let herself relax against his chest. He was here with her. For now. But would he stay?

CHAPTER NINE

THREE weeks later, Raphael tapped the front door of Annie's house before walking in. They had slipped into a comfortable pattern and there had been no more scares with the pregnancy, much to Annie's delight. As the door led straight into the small sitting room, Raphael found himself confronted with the sight of an inverted Annie. *Dios.* What was she doing?

Her upside-down face peered at him from the gap between her legs. She had tied her hair in a ponytail and it hung almost to the floor. She was wearing tight-fitting trousers that emphasised the shape of her bottom and her crop top revealed the taut mound of her belly and just the merest glimpse of the mound of her breasts. He felt something primeval stir in his belly.

'Oh, hello,' she said. 'I'm just doing a few

rounds of The Salute to the Sun. I'll be finished in a few moments.'

In a fluid movement she changed position, curving her sweet body through a series of movements. One minute he'd be staring at her delicious rear, the next he'd be watching as her toned arms took the weight of her body and she moved into a series of lunges. Eventually she stood upright and brought her hands together as if she were praying. He took in the tiny droplets of moisture on her skin, her face glowing with her exertions, the gentle rise and fall of her breasts. The swell of her pregnancy was outlined by her Lycra trousers. She had never looked so beautiful or so womanly to him before, and it took every ounce of his willpower not to pull her into his arms and run his tongue over her skin.

'Yoga,' she said, a small smile tugging at her lips. 'In case you are wondering. I've been doing it for years. And since it seems as if I am forbidden—' she looked at him with mock anger '—to do anything more strenuous, I've been practising every day.' She picked up a towel from her sofa and wiped the moisture from her skin. 'I find it helps me stay calm,' she added. 'And I'm hoping it will help me stay focused in labour.'

Raphael tore his eyes away. He loved the way her eyes sparkled with amusement. He hadn't seen Annie smile as often as he would have liked. More than anything, he wished he could be the one to bring the light to her face.

'I have come to ask you if you would like to come for a picnic. Catalina and Maria arrived last night and as it's a beautiful day, we thought Maria would like a trip to the beach. I know she would like it if you came too. Catalina also. She wants to meet the mother of her niece or nephew again.'

Dios, why had he said it in that way? Why couldn't he admit that he wanted to spend time with her, too? Because he couldn't, that was why. He had to remember that it didn't matter how much he wanted this woman back in his arms, an affair was out of the question. No woman was ever going to rip his heart out again. Not even this one. Especially not this one.

'Maria? Catalina?' She was frowning. A tiny pucker of her eyebrows. 'They are here? In Penhally Bay? To see me?' Annie wrapped the towel around her shoulders, hiding the exquisite swell of her breast from him.

'To see you, yes, but also because my mother had to go to the north of Spain to see her sister and she didn't want to take Maria with her. So she asked Catalina to take her for the weekend. My sister thought it was a chance to come here for a couple of days and get to know you a little. And Maria still talks about you. It would be a good chance to kill a bird with a stone, as you say in English.'

'Kill two birds with one stone,' Annie corrected him automatically. She wasn't looking as pleased as he'd thought she'd be. 'I don't know, Raphael. I'd like to see them both again, especially little Maria, but…' She tailed off.

Raphael could guess what she was thinking. He wondered if she had any idea how easily he was able to read her. She'd be worrying whether this was another attempt to persuade her to come and live in Spain.

'Please,' he said. 'I know I have no right to ask you. Your time is your own, but Maria would be so happy to see you again.'

He knew it was unfair of him to play the Maria

card. Annie might be able to resist a plea from him, but from the little girl? He doubted it. As soon as he saw the acceptance in her eyes he knew he had been right.

'Where are they?'

'I dropped them off at the beach. I told them I couldn't promise that you would come.'

'But you knew I would.' Annie quirked an eyebrow in his direction. She was right. He had been certain that she wouldn't be able to resist seeing Maria again.

'I'll just have a quick shower then change. You go on if you like. I'll walk down when I'm ready. It won't take long and I could do with the exercise.'

'I'll wait for you,' Raphael said, picking up one of the magazines he had brought over a few weeks ago, noting that they hadn't been read. What was wrong with Annie? Didn't she like motorbikes?

By the time they arrived at the beach, the sun was beating down and the beach was busy with locals making the most of the first really hot summer's day.

'In a couple of weeks the beach will be

crowded with tourists,' Annie told Raphael. 'We'll feel the impact at the hospital, too.'

'It is like Spain. In the winter everywhere is peaceful. Then the summer arrives and suddenly it doesn't feel like home any more.'

'I don't mind, though,' Annie protested. 'We're all tourists somewhere at some time. And I quite like the buzz when the visitors arrive.'

'Buzz?' Raphael repeated, looking perplexed.

Annie laughed. 'It's an expression. It means, an energy—an atmosphere.'

Raphael pointed to a couple of figures sitting on a blanket near the shelter of a wall.

'There they are. You go on while I find somewhere to change.'

Annie tiptoed across the hot sand, her sandals in her hand. As soon as Catalina saw her she jumped to her feet and hugged Annie.

'It is good to see you again.' She smiled. 'And looking so well. I trust my brother has been looking after you? Is everything all right now? He told us…' She tailed off.

'Everything's okay,' Annie said softly. 'I got a fright, but I'm okay now.'

Annie looked past Catalina's shoulder. Maria,

wearing her swimming costume, was standing watching Annie carefully, her thumb in her mouth.

'Hello, little one,' Annie said in Spanish. She had been swotting up some basic Spanish. As her child would almost certainly be bilingual, it seemed sensible.

The little girl broke into a shy smile and, stepping forward, wrapped her arms around Annie. Annie's heart squeezed as she ruffled Maria's thick dark curls.

'Where is my brother?' Catalina asked glancing over Annie's shoulder. 'Don't tell me he decided that he was needed at the hospital?'

'No. He's just getting changed.'

Suddenly Catalina grinned. 'Here he comes!'

Annie swung round. Raphael was striding towards them, wearing a wetsuit and carrying a surfboard. His bronzed chest was bare, the top half of his suit gathered around his lean hips. Annie could see the muscles in his upper arms bunch with the effort of carrying the board and she let her eyes slide down his body, taking in the toned six pack of his abdomen. The skin-tight fabric of his wetsuit clung to his thighs and across his hips. Annie's skin tingled.

As Maria ran towards him, short legs sending puffs of sand in her wake, he dropped the board and opened his arms. Maria careered into him and he pretended to be knocked over.

Annie watched them, regret vying with the feeling of lust. She was glad about the baby—more than glad. Why, then, did she feel this aching sense of loss?

Annie paddled with Maria while Raphael took his board to an area a little further along, which was cordoned off from bathers. Out of the corner of her eye she watched him as he rode the waves, his body bending and curving as he balanced. Every so often she would catch her breath as he disappeared from view, but seconds later he would reappear from under the wave still upright. He had surfed before, that much was obvious.

'I want to make a sandcastle,' Maria said after she had finished splashing about, so they left Raphael to make most of the waves and returned to where Catalina was setting out the picnic. Keeping a watchful eye on Maria as she played, the two women stretched out on the blanket.

'It is good to see my brother happy again,' Catalina said softly. 'It has been too long since I saw him laugh. I think being here, as well as you and the baby, has been good for him.'

'He told me about Sebastian, and Ruth,' Annie said softly. 'It must have been hard on him.'

'I have never seen him so…' Catalina paused. 'So distraught. He loved that little boy. You know, he left his room exactly how it was the day she took him. His toys on the bed, his football, everything, as if he expected him to come back. And he did expect him to come back, right up until the court case. When he knew he had lost Sebastian for ever, it was as though Raphael had lost part of himself.'

'What kind of woman was she, his ex-wife? I can't imagine anyone being so deceitful and then so cruel.'

'Ruth? I never liked her.' Catalina shrugged. 'She always seemed to me as if she thought herself above everyone. You know, before Raphael became a doctor he was a very good football player. He could have played professionally, but he decided to study medicine instead. I think she would have stayed if he had chosen a different profession. She wanted more money, a better lifestyle than a doctor could offer her. Raphael told her that he would never go back to football, that, apart from everything else, he was too old, but she never stopped trying to change his mind. Then she met Sebastian's father again. He is now a very important and rich man in Spain. She decided he could give her a better life. So she went, and took Sebastian with her.'

Maria had left her sandcastle and had come to sit next to Annie. She pressed her body into Annie's and Annie put her arm around the child, drawing her closer.

'He tried everything to get access, even just once a month, but he couldn't. I think it broke his heart. When he met you, he had just been at the lawyer to try one more appeal, but that failed, too.' Catalina looked at Annie thoughtfully. 'He was a good father. He will be a good father to your child. If you will let him.'

'I won't stop him seeing our child, Catalina. I wouldn't do that, not unless he gave me cause. But I worry sometimes that he will try and take our baby away from me. And I could never let that happen.'

Catalina looked Annie directly in the eyes. 'You are wrong to think like that. He would never do to you what has been done to him. Never. He knows a child needs a mother and a father. You have to believe me. Just be patient with him.'

Annie did believe her. She knew that she had been worried all along for nothing. Raphael wasn't the kind of man to remove a child from its mother. And if she hadn't been so scared she would have seen that before now.

Maria shifted in her arms and, putting a small hand up to Annie's face, turned it towards her.

'You are not sad any more?' she said

'No,' Annie replied, and included Catalina in her smile. 'I am not sad any more.'

The rest of the weekend sped past in a happy blur. Annie couldn't resist the entreaty in Maria's big brown eyes when Catalina suggested that Annie go with them to explore some of the hidden coves along the coast. As the four of them tramped along the beach, searching rock pools and underneath rocks for crabs, Annie let herself imagine what it would be like if this were *her* family. She saw the way Raphael was with Maria, the way he rolled up his jeans to paddle in the sea with her, the way he made the sad little girl giggle, and Annie's heart ached. If only he felt about her the way she felt about him. If only *they* could be a family.

She could no longer pretend that the way her heart hammered every time she saw him was simple lust. She loved him. With all her heart and soul. She had loved him from the moment she had met him and she would love him to the day she died. But, she reminded herself, even though the realisation almost cracked her heart in two, friendship was all he had to offer, and for the sake of their child it would have to be enough.

The following Monday, Annie was down at the Penhally Bay Surgery for a check-up with Kate when Nick popped his head around the door.

'Oh, I'm sorry. I didn't realise Kate still had someone with her. I'll come back in a few minutes.'

'No, come in,' Annie said. 'We're finished

here. I was just chatting to Kate before getting back to St Piran's for the clinic.'

'Actually, it's useful that you're here, Annie. The patient I wanted to talk to Kate about involves you too.'

He sat down opposite Kate and stretched his legs out in front of him. Annie didn't really know him that well. The older GP was always friendly and helpful, but there was a reticence about him that didn't really invite confidences. All Annie knew about him was that he was a widower with grown-up children and that he and Kate had worked together for a long time.

'I gather you saw Tilly Treliving a while back at the family planning clinic?' Nick said to Kate without preamble.

'Yes,' Kate replied. 'Is there a problem?'

'You could say that,' Nick said grimly. 'She's come to see me this morning. She's around thirty weeks pregnant, I think. If her dates are right.'

Kate looked shocked. 'She came to see me, let me see, almost a year ago about wanting to start a family, but I thought I'd agreed with her that we were going to get her diabetes stabilised first and that she would continue to use contraception until it settled down. I think Gemma has been following her up,' Kate said, referring to the practice nurse.

'Obviously she decided to go ahead anyway. It was only when Gemma became concerned that she hadn't been attending the surgery and went to visit her that we discovered the reason she'd been staying away.'

'Oh, poor Tilly. She must have been scared we'd tell her off,' Kate said.

'She'll need to be followed up at the hospital, of course,' Nick continued. 'I'm referring her to Dr Castillo. I'm just waiting for him to call me back. I gather he's in surgery, but if he isn't free to see her could you fit her in to one of your clinics, Annie?'

'Of course I'll see her,' Annie said. 'I'm down to do the afternoon clinic with Raphael. It would be no problem to add her on. But if she's still here, I could have a chat with her now, if you like. Unless you'd prefer to see her, Kate?'

'It sounds as if you'll be following her up, so it's probably best for you to see her,' Kate said. 'Besides, I'm due to visit a couple of my new mothers this afternoon. But let me know if there is anything I can do.'

A few moments after Kate and Nick had left, there was a soft tap at the door and a frightened-looking Tilly came into the room.

'It's all right, Tilly,' Annie said gently. 'I just need to do a few tests so we can see what's going on. Where's John? Couldn't he get time off work to come with you?'

'He's really angry with me.' The young woman burst into tears. 'We're barely speaking. He didn't want me to get pregnant. Not after what Kate told us.'

Annic handed Tilly a tissue and waited until the sobs tailed off. It wasn't great that Tilly had gone ahead and fallen pregnant, but she couldn't find it in her heart to blame her. She knew only too well how much the desperate desire to have a child could take over everything. But Tilly was taking a risk. Her diabetes could bring all sorts of complications for the baby as well as the mother.

'I'm sure John will come round. He's probably frightened for you, but we're going to take good care of you,' Annie said. 'Dr

Tremayne is going to speak to the obstetrician, Dr Castillo, at St Piran's. He specialises in pregnancies such as yours and will want to see you. He and I will follow you up at the hospital.'

'Won't Dr Castillo be angry with me too?' Tilly said. She had dried her eyes and was looking calmer. 'You promise you'll be with me when I see him?'

'Of course. But you mustn't worry about him being annoyed with you. He'll simply be concerned that we get you and the baby safely through the pregnancy. He's very kind, actually.'

Annie stood and went to fetch some more tissues. As she did, Tilly looked at her in surprise. 'Are you…?' she asked.

'Pregnant?' Annie finished for her. 'Yes, I am.'

'Oh, I didn't know you were married.'

'I'm not,' Annie said quietly.

Tilly looked embarrassed.

'Hey, it's okay,' Annie said.

'I don't care that I've put *my* health at risk,' the young woman said fiercely. 'I'm glad I'm going to have a baby. It's going to be loved.'

There was a tap on the door and Nick popped his head in. 'I've spoken to Dr Castillo,' he said.

'He's agreed to see Tilly at his clinic this after-noon, if she can manage that?'

'You can come with me in the car. I'm heading there myself. That way I can be with you when you see Dr Castillo. How does that sound?' There was no way Annie was going to give Tilly any opportunity to miss the appointment. Not when there was so much at risk.

Annie and Raphael saw Tilly together before the main clinic started. Raphael examined the young woman thoroughly before asking her to wait while he and Annie had a chat.

'I am not happy with her glucose levels, and the baby is already bigger than I would have expected for her dates. We are going to have to keep a close eye on her.'

Annie knew why he was concerned. Diabetic mothers often had problems in pregnancy and when the diabetes wasn't well controlled there was an increased risk of stillbirth. They would have to monitor her carefully and intervene just at the right time. It would be a tricky bal-ancing act.

'Don't worry,' Annie said. 'I intend to. Luckily

she stays in Penhally Bay, so I can pop in and see her from time to time.'

Raphael smiled broadly. 'Are you always so determined to get your patients safely through their pregnancies? Anyone would think you care about their babies almost as much as you do your own.'

Annie's heart flipped. Why did he have to be so gorgeous? Why did her hormonally loaded body react to him the way it did? But it wasn't her hormones. She had reacted this way to him from the moment she had met him, and she couldn't blame pregnancy hormones then. And the way he had been with Tilly. Kind, reassuring, not judgemental at all. It was a different, softer side to Raphael. And it just made her love him more.

'Speaking of your pregnancy, why don't we check your BP while we are waiting for the next patient to arrive?'

Before she could react he was wrapping a blood-pressure cuff around her arm.

'Hey, wait a minute,' Annie protested, alarmed to feel goose-bumps all along her arm where his fingers brushed her skin. 'Kate checked my blood pressure earlier. And it's fine. She's looking after me perfectly well. I wish you would stop treating me as if I were some walking incubator.'

Raphael narrowed his eyes at her. 'Is that what you think?' he said, amusement threading his voice.

'What else am I to think?' Annie said crossly. 'All you're interested in is the health and welfare of this baby.'

'Don't you think I'm interested in the health and welfare of the mother as well?' His eyes were unfathomable, but a smile tugged at the corner of his mouth. It was enough to make Annie's heart beat faster.

But before either of them could say more, the receptionist popped her head around the door to tell them that Claire and Roy had arrived to see them.

Annie watched as Raphael scanned Claire, who happily had no further bleeding. But as Raphael replaced the probe he had been using and Annie wiped away the lubricating gel from Claire's abdomen, Annie could tell that he was concerned.

He waited until Claire was dressed. As always Roy was there by her side. So far he hadn't missed a single appointment, even though Annie knew he had a demanding job that often took him away from home.

'The babies have grown since the last time I saw you,' Raphael said. 'But not as much as I would have liked.'

Claire's face paled and she clutched her husband's hand. The couple sat in silence, waiting for Raphael to continue.

'It's good that we have got the babies to over twenty-five weeks,' he continued. 'But now, I'm afraid, we have to make a decision.'

The couple nodded and waited for him to continue.

'We can continue to monitor the babies, and see how they progress, or we can deliver them now by Caesarean section. Both options carry a risk.' His voice was gentle. 'If we wait, it is possible that the smaller baby will die. If, on the other hand, we deliver them now, the smaller baby has an increased risk of not pulling through. The bigger baby also has greater risk of complications as all pre-term babies do.'

Claire and Roy absorbed the information silently, but Annie could see the fear etched on their faces.

'What would you do?' Roy asked Raphael. 'If it were your babies we were talking about?'

'I'm afraid this has to be your decision,' Raphael replied softly.

'Which option carries more risk for Claire? However much we want these babies, it is her that matters most.'

'Neither option is more or less risky for your wife,' Raphael said. 'Whatever you decide, it is more than likely that Claire will require a C-section. Any operation carries a small risk, but many, many women have this procedure every day without harm.'

Roy looked at Annie. She could see the tension in his face. The love he felt for his wife was written there plain for the world to see. 'What would you do, Annie?'

Annie shook her head. She didn't know what she would do if she were in their shoes. It wasn't a question she could answer.

'Both options carry a risk,' she replied. 'If we leave Claire, there is a chance the second, smaller twin could die suddenly in utero. The bigger twin would continue to grow and every day spent inside Claire's tummy increases its chances of being born healthy. If we chose to deliver both twins now, the bigger one will probably do okay, though there is still the chance of complications, but the second, smaller twin is more likely to struggle, because they are twins they are already smaller than they would be for their gestation. I'm guessing—' Annie turned to Raphael for confirmation '—from what we can see on the scan that the smaller baby is closer to twenty weeks' size.'

'So essentially you are saying that, whatever we do, we could lose either one or both of our children.' Although Roy's voice was calm, Annie could see that he was finding it difficult not to break down in front of his wife. Once again she marvelled at the very real love between this couple. Beside him, Claire was crying quietly. 'How are we supposed to decide what to do?' Roy continued.

'If I were you,' Raphael said, 'I would wait another week or two.' Annie looked at him, surprised. After everything he had said about not wanting to make a decision for the couple, here he was doing just that. But as she caught his eye, she knew what he was thinking. Waiting gave the couple a better chance of one healthy child.

'Essentially, what Dr Castillo is saying is that if you do nothing right now, you have a better chance of having one normal child. But there is a greater risk of the second twin dying in utero. If you go ahead and have a section today then the second twin could still die, and the bigger one still has a chance of complications. But there is a chance both could survive.'

'I don't want either of my babies to die,' Claire cried. 'I love them both. I can't sacrifice one for the other.'

'We will go along with whatever you decide, of course,' Raphael said. 'I just wanted to make sure you understand the options.'

'Thank you for your frankness, Dr Castillo,' Roy said quietly. 'I wonder if my wife and I could have a moment to discuss it?'

'You don't have to make up your minds right now,' Annie interjected. 'Go home. Have a think about it. Then let us know.'

'From what you tell us, every day we delay is a day that one of our babies could die. No, I think we need to decide now, today. We just need some time.' He looked up at Annie and she recoiled from the naked pain in his eyes. She had grown fond of the couple and she would have given anything in her power to make everything all right for them. But it wasn't in her power, she admitted sadly as she followed Raphael out of the room, leaving Claire in Roy's arms. They had done everything they could.

In the staff room Raphael turned to face Annie.

'Are you okay?' he asked gently.

Annie nodded glumly. 'I just wish we could wave a magic wand and make everything all right for them. They want this so much.' Her voice broke and before she knew it Raphael had pulled her into his arms. She leaned her head against his chest as he stroked her hair.

'You shouldn't take every case so much to heart, *cariño*.'

She let herself relax in his arms. Here it felt as if nothing bad could ever happen to her, or to anyone else. In his arms she felt as if she'd come home. Reluctantly, she eased herself away from him. She had to remember that all he was offering her was friendship. Even if her beating heart reminded her that she wanted so much more.

Raphael looked down at her, his dark eyes glowing, and Annie caught her breath. She knew she must be mistaken, but he was looking at her as if…as if he wanted to kiss her. The air fizzled and crackled between them, just as it had the night they'd met, and Annie felt her world tilt.

Before either of them could move, Roy appeared at the door, mercifully oblivious to the atmosphere in the room.

'We've made our decision,' he said.

Back inside the consulting room, Claire had dried her tears and was sitting pale-faced but composed.

'We are going to take Dr Castillo's advice and wait,' she said calmly, looking Annie directly in the eyes. 'I know we might lose one this way, but we have waited so long to have children we just can't take the chance of losing them both. It's not about whether they'll have problems, I will love my children regardless and with Roy and his family's support we would cope. No, it's the thought that if I have a section now, I could lose both my children. I cannot risk that.'

'For what it's worth,' Raphael said, 'I think it's the right decision. But I'm going to suggest you attend day-care clinic twice a week so we can monitor you. I know it will be difficult for you, but it means if there is a sudden change we can act quickly.'

'I think you're being very brave,' Annie added. 'It's an impossible decision, but we are going to do everything we can to see you through it.' Glancing up, she caught the gleam of approval in Raphael's eyes. Almost imperceptibly he nodded at her. But it wasn't that she necessarily agreed with him, it was simply that the couple having made up their minds needed her full support. She just hoped for all their sakes that they had made the right choice.

CHAPTER TEN

ALMOST imperceptibly, Annie and Raphael developed a routine. Every evening, when he wasn't on call, Raphael would call at the cottage and after he had interrogated her about her health they would go for a walk down to the harbour. They would talk about Spain and Penhally Bay and places they had been on holiday. Everything, it seemed, except what was going to happen once the baby was born. But Annie didn't want to spoil the fragile peace between them. They discovered a shared love of opera and Annie admitted she loved country and western music and Raphael teased her about it. He told her that he played the guitar sometimes for the flamenco dancers for which his home town was famous.

'You must come back to Spain,' he said. 'There is so much I want to show you.'

Whenever he suggested it, which was often, Annie would smile. 'Of course I'll want to bring him or her to Spain. I want my child to grow up knowing about all their family.'

The evenings were getting lighter every day as her bump grew larger. Annie saw Kate at the surgery for her check-ups and the senior midwife declared herself happy with Annie's progress. Her baby was due at the end of September and towards the end of June, Annie decided that it was time to prepare the nursery. If she waited much longer she'd never be able to balance on the stepladder.

And that was where Raphael found her one evening when she was up the ladder, painting the wall of the soon-to-be nursery.

'Come down at once,' he said crossly. He had stopped waiting for Annie to open the door to him and would just come in after a brief warning knock.

'Whatever for? I've still a good half of the wall to do.' She carried on painting. 'If you want to help, grab a brush from over there.' As she indicated the brushes and paint for the wall, the ladder wobbled and Annie almost lost her balance. But in a flash Raphael was up the ladder, steadying her against him.

'Be careful, *cariño*,' he said. 'Please come down.'

'Hey, I'm okay. I just lost my balance for a moment. I wouldn't have fallen.' But Raphael clearly wasn't in the mood for an argument. He picked her up and lifted her down from the ladder. He held her tight against him and she could feel the thudding of his heart through the thin cotton of his T-shirt. Her body melted into his, at least as far as her abdomen would let her, and his arms moved down her body, pressing her closer. Annie felt dizzy with desire. Before she could help herself her arms snaked around his neck and she was lifting her face to his.

Gently he disentangled her arms from around his neck and stood back.

'I don't think it would be a good idea,' he said.

Annie was mortified. What on earth had got into her? Given the slightest bit of encouragement, she would have kissed him. It was what she longed to do. It was what she had been longing to do for weeks now, she realised with a thud of her heart. It didn't matter what she told herself, she found him as devastatingly gorgeous and sexy as the day she had first met him. She had tried to pretend that she didn't but she could no longer hide it from herself. Or from him, she thought ruefully. There was no mistaking her intent—at least not for a man as experienced as Raphael.

'No,' she said shortly. 'I can see that a heavily pregnant woman might not be everyone's cup of tea.'

'Mierda,' he groaned under his breath. 'You should see yourself. I doubt there is a woman in the world who looks more beautiful than you do right now. But it is not right. We have to be sensible. What is the point in having sex—no matter how much I would like to—when we are just becoming friends?'

Regardless of what he said, Annie felt rejected. Did he think she was trying to seduce him, to force him into a deeper relationship?

'I'm sorry,' she said stiffly. 'I don't know what I was thinking.' Then she tried a smile to ease some of the tension. 'They do say some women react like that to pregnancy hormones. I'm clearly one of them.'

Raphael looked at her quizzically then opened his mouth as if he were about to say something. But then he seemed to change his mind and picked up a paintbrush.

'I will finish this,' he said. 'You put your feet up and rest.'

'I'm not tired! In fact, I feel great. I'll make us something to eat,' she said.

By the time she returned from the kitchen to tell him the meal was ready, Raphael had finished the room. He stood back and surveyed his work, looking decidedly pleased with himself.

'I wonder what it will be. A boy or a girl.'

'We'll just have to wait to find out,' Annie teased.

Raphael wiped his hand across his forehead, leaving a yellow streak of paint behind. Impulsively, Annie stood on tiptoe to wipe away the smear.

Raphael reached up and trapped her hand in his. He brought her hand to his lips and kissed her fingers, sending a jolt of electricity all the way to her toes. Before she knew it, he was kissing her. Deep, searching kisses as if he wanted to possess her very soul. But even as she felt herself melt in his arms, Annie knew it was a mistake. Breathlessly she pulled away. They stood looking at each other. Before either of them could speak, Raphael's pager bleeped. He looked at the number and frowned. 'It's the hospital. Can I use your phone?'

As soon as he replaced the phone a little later, Annie knew something was up.

'It's Claire,' he said. 'She's gone into labour. I need to go to the hospital. I promised her I would do her section.'

'I'm coming with you,' Annie said, picking up her jacket.

'Of course. I know they both want you there.'

As they drove, they discussed Claire.

'At least she's made it to twenty-eight weeks,' Annie said as Raphael negotiated the narrow lanes to the hospital. Annie had been present when Raphael had scanned Claire the day before. Everyone had been relieved to see the second twin's heart was still beating strongly.

'Yes. It's better than I hoped or expected.'

'The twins will need to spend a few weeks in Special Care. But let's just hope the second twin survives.'

Too busy concentrating on the road, Raphael didn't reply.

As soon as they arrived at the hospital they rushed down to theatre and were ready and waiting by the time Claire was wheeled in with an apprehensive Roy at her side.

Annie bent over the mother to be and smiled reassuringly. 'You'll be a mum soon,' she whispered.

Claire looked up at her with frightened eyes. 'I'm scared, Annie. So scared.'

'Everything will be okay,' Annie said. 'You've done really well to have managed this far. And both hearts are beating strongly. We'll need to take your babies up to Special Care as soon as they are delivered. But we'll let you see them as soon as we can. Okay?'

As soon as Claire's spinal block was working, Raphael made his first incision. It wasn't the first time Annie had seen him operate, but she never tired of the way his brow furrowed as he concentrated. He operated quickly, without wasting any time. Within minutes he was removing the bigger of the twins. As Annie stepped forward to take the girl from Raphael she was pleased to note that the first baby was a good size and, as it gave a loud cry, with a good set of lungs. The second twin was a little boy, and was more of a concern. He was very small and Annie knew that his parents were in for weeks of worry while his lungs developed fully. Very briefly, as promised, Annie showed Claire and Roy their babies before handing them over to the paediatrician.

'They're both so tiny,' Claire whispered.

'They both have a good chance, Claire,' Annie said. 'They'll look after them upstairs. I'll take you up to see them as soon as possible.'

Claire looked from Annie to Raphael, tears glistening in her eyes.

'Thank you,' she whispered.

Annie smiled back. She had a good feeling about the twins.

Later, after they had left Claire and Roy, Raphael drove them both back to Annie's house. Neither of them spoke, each too preoccupied with their thoughts. Annie thought back to the kiss they had shared. She had known that she loved him, had known from the day she had met him that she loved him, she just hadn't been able to admit it to herself. Whatever she had felt for Robert, it had come no where near the feelings she had for Raphael. Whenever he was near every atom in her body seemed to come alive, and when he wasn't there she missed him desperately.

She sneaked a glance at him from under her lashes. He was like the missing piece of the jigsaw that was her life. But it was no use. Although he was attracted to her, he didn't love her. And Annie would never again be with someone who didn't feel about her the way she felt about them. Whatever pain lay in store for her, she would have to deal with it. Even though it would be torture to see him, share her child with him, stand by while he married someone else, she had no choice. As long as he wanted to be part of their child's life, she would have to let him. She just had to make sure he never guessed how she felt about him.

The days passed and Annie felt well and continued to revel in feeling the life growing inside her. Although she still had a few weeks to go, she was happy that everything was ready for the baby. Raphael had finished painting the nursery and he had assembled the cot, with her passing him the tools, much in the same way as she passed him instruments in theatre. At the hospital they worked together often and had developed an easy understanding of how each other worked. Raphael's reputation was spreading and more and more patients, especially those with high-risk pregnancies, were asking to see him.

After her clinic one morning, Annie went in search of Raphael and she found him in the doctors' lounge, chatting with Ben Carter.

As soon as Raphael spotted her he stood and went across to her. He touched her hand. 'What is it, Annie? Are you okay?' His concern never ceased to touch her, although she knew it was mainly for his unborn child. They still hadn't spoken about what would happen after the birth. For the time being, Annie was content to let things ride.

'I've just seen Tilly down at the clinic. I wanted her to see you, but she wouldn't stay.'

'What's going on with her?' Raphael asked. 'Her blood-glucose control was terrible the last time we saw her. I had hoped she would have managed to bring it under control with changes to her diet and increasing her insulin.'

'That's just it. Her glucose profile was even worse today and the baby is much bigger than it should be for her dates.'

Raphael chewed his lip, looking thoughtful. 'Does her partner come with her?'

'He wasn't here today.'

'It would be useful to know what he thinks,' Raphael said. 'Tell you what, why don't I call in on them on my way home tonight? Would that help, do you think?'

Annie was relieved. She couldn't explain it but she felt really uneasy about Tilly. The young woman wasn't looking after herself and Annie knew she would be devastated if she lost her baby. Why wasn't she looking after herself better? Was it simply that Annie and Raphael hadn't managed to get across how crucial this was for the health of her baby?

'We should both go,' Annie said. 'I'll meet you there after work. Say about sixish. Would that be okay?'

'I have an elective section this afternoon after

my main list is finished. But I should be able to make it, if everything goes according to plan. Which it will do.' He grinned down at her.

Her heart flipped. There was something so supremely confident about Raphael. In another man it might have come across as arrogance, but in him it was simple recognition of his own ability.

'But before theatre I have a postnatal ward round to do,' he continued. 'Are you joining me?'

Annie watched as Raphael went to see each of his patients. Each woman got the same attention, as if she were the most important person in the world to him right at that moment. If someone's baby was crying, Raphael would pick it up and rock it in his arms while he talked to the woman. He always managed to find some compliment for each baby that left the mother smiling with pride, believing her baby to have been singled out for particular praise. But it wasn't an act. Annie could see he was genuinely interested. It was a different side to Raphael, one she had seen countless times since he had come to work at St Piran's but it never ceased to surprise her. How much more tender he would be with his own child she could only guess at.

'I thought Spanish men were too macho to coo over babies,' she teased him as they made their way out of the ward.

'Coo?' He looked at her, puzzled. 'What is this coo? It doesn't sound very nice.'

'Fuss. That's what it means,' Annie replied.

'Spanish men love children,' he said. 'We don't see them as inconveniences to be hidden away, like some countries. I would like a whole brood of them one day. A football team—or at least a five-a-side.'

Annie felt her heart crack a little. It was another reason why she and Raphael would never be anything except co-parents. The baby she was carrying was enough of a miracle. There would never be any more for her.

Annie knocked on the door of Tilly's small cottage but there was no reply. It was strange. She had telephoned after speaking to Raphael to warn her that they would be calling in around six. Perhaps Tilly had popped out to the shops?

She knocked again and then tried the door, and was surprised to find it unlocked. She opened it and walked in. The residents sometimes left their doors unlocked in the winter, but with the influx of tourist at this time of year, people tended to be more careful. The house didn't feel empty. Music was playing on the radio and there was a bag of unpacked shopping at the door, as if it had been abandoned. Immediately Annie felt alarm bells ringing. She stepped further into the house, calling out Tilly's name. Perhaps she had gone for a bath? But then as soon as she entered the sitting room she saw her. Tilly was lying on the floor, unmoving, and Annie rushed to her side, dropping to her knees. The young woman was unconscious and Annie made sure Tilly was breathing before pushing her over on her side into the recovery position. She smelt for the distinctive odour of ketones, but it wasn't there. Tilly must be having a hypo. So she needed to get sugar in to her system. Quickly, she rummaged in her bag. Did she still have the glucose gel she kept for emergencies? Thankfully, she discovered it hidden under a glucose test kit—she'd need that too. Taking a generous dollop from the container she spread the gel inside Tilly's lips, hoping the sugar would be absorbed rapidly.

She wondered how long Tilly had been lying

unconscious. Where was John? Shouldn't he be home by now? And where was Raphael? She could do with his help. She bent over Tilly, pricking her finger with the stylet from the testing kit. Her glucose was dangerously low, no wonder she was unconscious. She needed to get her to hospital. She was digging in her shoulder bag for her mobile when she heard Raphael's voice calling out her name.

He stood there, taking in the scene with a glance.

'I found her here like this just a couple of minutes ago. She's having a bad hypo. I've put some glucose gel on her lips, but so far it's having no effect and I haven't had a chance to check the baby yet. I was just about to call for an ambulance when you arrived.'

'What about glucagon?' he said, crouching beside Annie and checking Tilly's pulse. 'We teach all the diabetic mothers to use it an emergency. She must a keep a syringe of it somewhere handy.' He took the Sonicaid Annie held out to him. 'I'll check the foetal heart while you see if you can find it.'

'Shouldn't I phone for an ambulance first?'

'No, if we can get some glucagon into her

that'll buy us the time we need. She could do with a drip, too.'

'Found it!' Annie exclaimed, taking the cover off the pre-filled syringe and plunging the needle into Tilly's leg. Thankfully she had left it in full view on the side table.

'She should come round quickly now,' Raphael said, and sure enough Tilly groaned. Over her stirring form Raphael and Annie smiled at each other. Their eyes locked and Annie felt her world spin on its axis. He was looking at her as if… Then his eyes seemed to lose their warmth—as if she was a professional he admired, she admonished herself. Nothing more.

'We still need to get her to hospital. The baby seems fine, but her diabetes is so badly controlled I'm not sure we should let the pregnancy continue much longer. She's thirty-five weeks. Maybe it's just as well to get her delivered.'

'I need to find out what's going on with her when we get her to hospital,' Annie said. 'I know how much she wants this baby so for her to be taking chances with her health like this seems out of character.'

'There will be time for that later. I agree it's

important, but right now we have to make sure that the baby stays healthy long enough to be delivered. I suggest that once she comes round completely, we put her in the back of my car and take her there ourselves. If that's okay with you?'

Annie nodded. She'd feel happier once she knew that Tilly was in hospital where she could be properly looked after.

Tilly stirred and her eyes focused gradually on Annie. 'Where am I? What happened? Where's John?' She tried to sit up, her eyes frantically searching the room. As soon as she realised John wasn't there she sank back down and began to cry quietly. 'He didn't come back, did he? He's never coming back. What am I going to do?'

'Hush, Tilly,' Annie soothed. 'You slipped into a hypo, but you and your baby are all right now. Dr Castillo is here and we're going to take you to hospital. We can find John later. You can phone him from the ward.'

'You don't understand,' Tilly wailed. 'He's not coming back. He doesn't want me or the baby.' And then as Annie put her arms around the heaving shoulders of her distressed patient, Tilly sobbed as if her heart would break.

By the time they had Tilly settled in the ward it was almost eight. Annie was feeling tired and hungry. She and Raphael agreed that they would wait until the next day before making a decision whether or not to deliver Tilly's baby early.

'She's thirty-five weeks,' Raphael said as they made their way to his car. 'Obviously I'd prefer to wait another couple of weeks but I don't think we can afford to take the risk.'

'At least these days a thirty-five-weeker has an excellent chance of doing well. I agree with you, the longer we wait the riskier for Tilly's baby.'

Raphael opened the door of his car for Annie and helped her in. As she sat back in the leather seat Annie yawned. 'I think I'll go straight to bed,' she said. 'I'm too exhausted even to think about cooking.' Raphael looked at her sharply but slid the car into gear without saying anything.

'I wish Tilly had told me she and John were having problems,' Annie said. 'I would have kept a closer eye on her had I known.'

'What kind of man leaves his partner to cope with a pregnancy on her own?' Raphael said savagely. 'Especially when he knows there are difficulties.'

'From what she told us, they had been having problems for a while. That's why she got pregnant. She thought it would bring them back together. Poor girl.'

'Irresponsible, you mean,' Raphael said. 'Gambling with her own health as well as the health of her baby.'

'I don't think you can be too hard on her,' Annie said. 'She loves John and she really wants this baby. Sometimes we all do things that aren't completely rational. At least, I do. Can you say you've never done anything that wasn't logically thought out?'

He turned his head towards her and looked as if he were about to say something then thought better of it. 'I just wish people would realise that a baby isn't an accessory,' he said. 'That they are a commitment for life. Not just something you have on a whim.'

Annie heard the underlying bitterness to his words and knew he was thinking about Sebastian.

'It is not our job to be judgemental,' Annie insisted. 'Our job is to ensure a healthy baby at the end. Just that. And if that means getting involved with their lives to make sure of that outcome, it's all part of the job. At least, that's the way I see it.' Annie broke off, aware that she sounded heated. But to her, patients weren't just pregnant women, they were women with lives, women like Tilly with relationship problems, women like her who had to balance motherhood with a career, women who had financial worries, and all of that had to be taken into consideration.

Raphael pulled up outside her house and switched off the ignition. 'You really care about them all, don't you?' he said. 'They all matter.' He looked into the distance and Annie could see the lines of tiredness creasing his eyes—or was it sadness? 'But what about the fathers?' he continued softly. 'Don't they have rights too? Don't they play an important part?' He laughed mirthlessly. 'Or do we exist just to provide the sperm?'

Annie turned to Raphael. 'I know your wife hurt you badly,' she said, 'but not every woman is like her. Most of us just want…' She hesitated. 'Most of us want a loving relationship, someone to share the ups and downs of life. And if a baby is part of that…so much the better.' She had to force herself to look at him. 'I know we got it the wrong way round. In an ideal world, I would be having a baby with someone who loved me.' A muscle twitched in his jaw as he studied her intently. He looked as far away from Annie as she had ever seen him. 'But at least I know my baby will have a father who will cherish him. Who will, I know, be there for him. And when it comes down to it, that is the most important thing of all.'

Suddenly the clouds vanished from his eyes. 'What is important that you eat and then get some rest. Come on, let's see what you have in that fridge. I may not be any good at making toast but I can cook a great frittata.'

Annie thought about protesting. She didn't know whether she had the energy to deal with Raphael in her house. It was hard enough to hide the way she felt about him at work, but alone with him, with her guard down? The last thing she wanted was for him to guess, if, God forbid, he hadn't already done so. But Raphael was already out of the car and was holding her door open.

'I won't take no for an answer,' he said firmly. 'You're tired. Making you something to eat is the least I can do.'

He stretched out a hand and Annie had no choice but to take it. As she felt his hand wrap around hers she felt a warmth suffuse her body. It would be so good to have someone who cared about her. Someone who wanted this baby as much as she did, because they had deliberately made it out of love. But that wasn't going to happen. But just this once, just for tonight, even if it was only inside her head, couldn't she pretend that they were a normal couple looking forward to the birth of their baby, knowing they had the rest of their lives to look forward to?

'I want to do something for you.' He looked at her intently. 'Please?'

She couldn't refuse the look of entreaty in his deep brown eyes.

'Okay,' she said. 'I give in. Just as long as it is better than the breakfast you made me.'

Annie showered, leaving Raphael to rummage around in her kitchen for the ingredients for a meal. By the time she returned, delicious smells of bacon and garlic were wafting through the kitchen.

'What can I do?' she asked.

'Nothing. Just sit there and look beautiful,' Raphael replied, settling her into an armchair.

'I'm not ill, you know,' she protested, but she couldn't stop a smile from creeping across her face. He had called her beautiful. Did he really think so, or was it just part of the patter he gave every woman? The thought wiped the smile off her face. Don't think about that just now, she told herself. Just enjoy being here with him tonight.

After they had eaten—and Raphael was right, the frittata was delicious—Raphael made them some coffee. They sat in companionable silence for a while.

'What are you hoping for?' Raphael asked suddenly. 'A boy or a girl?'

'Oh, I don't mind. I'm just so happy to be having a baby at all. As long as it's healthy…' She laughed. 'You know, when mothers used to say that, I wasn't ever sure whether I believed them or not. Now I know that they meant it.' Suddenly she felt a kick just below her ribs. 'Oops,' she said. 'The way this one is kicking, I think we may have a footballer on our hands.'

In a flash, Raphael was off his chair and on his knees beside her. He looked up, searching her eyes. 'Can I feel?' he asked.

She nodded, suddenly breathless. He placed his hand gently on her stomach, just as the baby gave another vigorous kick. As she looked down on Raphael's bent head, she was tempted to place her hand on his thick curls and run her fingers through his hair. It took all her willpower to resist the impulse. Especially when he looked up at her and she saw the tenderness in his eyes.

'I would like a girl,' he said. 'One who looks just like you. A girl who is just like you.'

Her breath caught in her throat. He reached up and took her hand, kissing each finger in turn. The pressure of his lips was an exquisite pain and every bit of her cried out to be taken in his arms and kissed senseless.

Slowly he rose to her feet and pulled her upright. Then she was in his arms and he was kissing her. Unsure, she pulled away slightly but as he held her closer, dropping his hands to her hips, there was no mistaking his desire for her. She closed her eyes and gave in to the feelings shooting around her body. If he hadn't been holding her, she didn't think her legs could have kept her upright.

Suddenly he pulled away. He was breathing deeply, his eyes black with desire. She almost whimpered when she felt him release her.

'*Mierda,*' he said. 'It is not good to make love. Not now.'

But then she was back in his arms. His hands were on her breasts, his touch sending hot f ashes of need to her groin. Slowly he pulled open her dressing gown, revealing her bra and panties and her swollen belly. She covered her belly with her hands, feeling shy.

'Let me see,' he demanded. 'Don't you know how beautiful you are to me, especially now, with my baby growing inside you?'

He eased the dressing gown off her shoulders and lowered her onto the rug beside the fire, the flickering light playing across his features. He dipped a hand under her bra and she felt her nipples tighten in response. Why was he doing this? He had just said they couldn't make love. Then his hand reached behind her back and he undid the clip of her bra. Her breasts sprang free and he cupped them, his thumbs circling her nipples sending shock waves of pleasure through her.

'Ah,' he said, a smile on his lips 'But I didn't say there weren't other ways of making love that would be safe for the baby.' He trailed a hand down over her stomach. His hand rested there for a moment, then he lowered his head and took one of her nipples into his mouth. Annie was lost. She could no more have stopped him than she could have carried an elephant on her back. Every touch of his fingers made her want more. The sensations in her body were overpowering. She knew it wouldn't be long before she had to give in, but at the same time she never ever wanted him to stop doing what he was doing.

His hand resting on her belly slid lower until it was resting just at the top of her panties. He pulled his head away and looked into her eyes. 'Do you want me to stop?' he asked. She shook her head, unable to speak. She had just enough time to see the triumph in his eyes before he was slipping his hand under the silk and between her legs. Then she was moving against him, unable to prevent her body's response to his touch. Then slowly, as he touched her gently at first, then with increasing pressure and pace, she felt her body explode with pleasure and she cried his name.

Eventually the world steadied around them and Raphael held her in his arms as her breathing returned to normal. She wondered at his self-control, that he could have the restraint to love her without asking anything in return. All of a sudden she felt shy again. She reached over and undid his belt and he groaned as she touched him lightly with her fingers and pulled her closer.

'You don't have to,' he said, as if the words physically hurt him.

'But I want to,' Annie said quietly. She knelt over him and undid the buttons of his jeans, then they were off and he was lying naked beside her. Remembering from the night they had met, she touched him the way he liked it, teasing him, slowing down, sometimes stopping when she sensed he was near then starting again. Then when she knew he couldn't take much more she used both her hands until he, holding her in a vice-like grip, gave in to his own climax.

Later they lay in each other's arms. Annie laid

her head on the smoothness of Raphael's chest where she could hear the steady thump, thump of his heart. His hands stroked her hair, smoothing it away from her eyes.

'Will you marry me, Annie?' he said.

Annie sat bolt upright. She felt a zing of happiness course through her veins. He wanted to marry her. He must feel the same way she did. The connection they had felt that first night was still there; it hadn't gone away.

'Pardon?' she said, wanting to make sure she had heard him right. 'What did you say.'

He sat up, grinning at her. The light bounced off his bronzed skin. She had never thought him so sexy as she did right them. She knew she loved every inch of him. His thoughtfulness, his humour, even his old-fashioned masculinity, and he loved her! It was almost too much to take in. She had resigned herself to never finding someone who loved her the way she needed to be loved. Wholeheartedly, without reservation, and now, just when she had thought she couldn't be happier…

'We could live in Spain. You, me and the baby. Be a family,' he said. 'A real family.'

An icy shiver ran up Annie's spine. She couldn't help but notice that he hadn't said he loved her.

'Live in Spain? But my job is here, my parents, my friends,' she said quietly. If he loved her, surely he'd be prepared to be wherever she was?

'You would be part of my family. My mother would welcome you like her own daughter. She will love you. I am sure of it.'

But still he hadn't said *he* loved her.

'And as for your job, you don't need to work. I have plenty of money and besides a woman should be at home with her child, no?' He continued, seemingly oblivious to her silence, 'Of course, then there will be no need to go to the lawyers for access.'

She was furious. She stood, picking up her discarded dressing gown and pulling it on over her shoulders.

'So that is what this is about,' she said through clenched teeth. 'My God, Raphael, is there nothing you wouldn't do to get your own way? Had you planned this all along? Did you really think that after you made love to me, I'd be so grateful that I would go along with your plans?

Was this the only way left to get your child with you in Spain? And if the price you have to pay for that is marriage to a woman you don't really love, then so be it.'

She picked up his jeans and T-shirt and flung them at him. 'But what about what I want? Did that cross your mind? Please don't imagine for one minute that I would enter into a loveless marriage, no matter how convenient.'

If she hadn't been so angry she might have laughed at the bewilderment on Raphael's face as he slipped on his T-shirt and jeans. But she was in no mood for laughing. How could she have let her guard down? She knew how much Raphael wanted this baby and she had completely underestimated the lengths he would go to to get what he wanted.

'Let yourself out,' she said. 'I'm going to bed.'

CHAPTER ELEVEN

AFTER leaving Annie's, Raphael decided to go for a walk on the beach. He was far too restless to go to sleep and he needed time to think. He always thought better when he was doing something. He had thought about following her into the bedroom and trying to explain, but something told him that Annie was in no mood to listen to him, let alone believe him. *Dios*, he thought ruefully, she is like a tiger when she is angry. He had never seen her other than quiet and calm, but he didn't find the new side to Annie off-putting. He was delighted that there was still lots more to find out about her. And whatever she thought right now, he fully intended that they would have time to discover each other.

The night sky was shot with lilac. Until

recently he had wondered if he had done the right thing coming here. He thought back to the day he had met Annie. He had been hurting then, and the pain he had seen reflected in her eyes had drawn him to her. It hadn't just been her beauty, although with her pale skin and light green eyes and that luscious body, there was no denying he had been powerfully attracted to her. So attracted he hadn't been able to stop himself taking her to bed, even though he had known in his soul that it was dangerous. And he had been right. But she had turned out to be dangerous in a way he couldn't have possibly imagined.

When he'd found out she was pregnant he hadn't been sure she was telling him the truth. After all, he had been deceived before. But the more he learned about her, the more he knew that she didn't have a deceitful bone in her body. She was too transparent for a start. He wondered if she realised how every emotion showed on her face—he always knew what she was thinking. But the worst thing of all was he knew he was falling in love with her. He couldn't stop thinking about her, he couldn't stop himself remembering how she had felt in his arms. Her soft, silky skin, the smell of her perfume, the way the pulse beat at the base of her throat, the way her thick hair fell across his face when they were making love covering him in her scent. And it wasn't just a physical attraction he felt any longer. If it had been he knew he would have been able to deal with that. It was her innate kindness, her laugh, the way she smiled, her mouth curving at the corners, and the way her eyes sparkled when she was happy.

He groaned aloud and, picking up a pebble, he threw it into the sea where it skipped over the waves. It was too late. He wasn't *falling* in love with her. He already loved her. With a passion. All he had to do now was persuade her that he meant it.

After Raphael left, Annie made herself a cup of tea, still fuming. How could she have been so naïve? She rubbed her back. She'd had a dull ache all day and now it was getting worse. A flicker of fear shot through her as her abdomen cramped. Dear God, no! She couldn't be going into labour. It was far too early. She was only twenty-eight weeks.

'Okay,' she told herself. 'Keep calm.' It could be Braxton-Hicks contractions, couldn't it? Or a tummy bug. It was one thing being a trained midwife and being able to reassure her patients, but quite another being the patient herself. She looked at her watch. Ten o'clock. It was late, but Kate or Chloe would probably still be awake. She could phone one of them, just for reassurance. She could also phone Raphael, of course, but she quickly dismissed the thought. Right now he was the last person she wanted to speak to. She had told him she could cope perfectly well without him so she could hardly call him every time she felt a twinge.

Making up her mind, she phoned Kate. Happily she hadn't gone to bed, but straight away Kate picked up on Annie's anxiety.

'What is it, Annie?' she said. 'Is something wrong?'

'It's probably nothing,' Annie said. 'But I've been having some lower back pain and some cramping. I'm probably being over-anxious, but I just wondered…' As she said the words a sharp tight pain squeezed her abdomen and she gasped.

'I'm coming,' Kate said. 'But first I'm going

to call an ambulance. Only as a precaution. Just hold on, Annie, I'll be there in ten minutes.'

Now Annie was seriously frightened. If Kate was calling for an ambulance, she must be worried too. But they had to be wrong. She couldn't be going into labour. She just couldn't. It was far too early. But Annie knew that it was entirely possible. The chances of premature labour had slightly increased after she'd had the miscarriage scare. Kate would know that, too. It was probably why she had called the ambulance. She sat down as another wave of pain washed through her body. She wrapped her arms around her body, almost as if by doing so she could keep her baby safe inside her. If she was going into labour she needed to get to hospital, perhaps there they could give her something to stop it. Every day the baby stayed safe in her womb was crucial at this point.

Unaware of how much time had passed since she had called Kate, she was relieved when she heard a knock on the door. Thank God, she thought. Kate had arrived. Maybe everything would still be okay.

* * *

Raphael had decided to go back and see Annie. Whatever she said, they needed to talk. He had to tell her how he felt.

But one look at her, curled up in the armchair, her eyes wild with terror, was enough to send his heart crashing against his ribs.

Before he could breathe he was by her side.

'What is it, Annie?' he said, taking in her pale face and pinched lips.

She moaned and clutched her stomach. 'The baby,' she gasped. 'I think it's coming.'

She reached out a hand and gripped his arm. 'Make it stop, Raphael. It's too early, please make it stop. I can't lose my baby. You have to help me.'

Raphael forced his own fear away. He needed to be strong for Annie right now.

'Tell me,' he said gently.

'I've been having backache all day, but it was different from before. I just thought I had strained a muscle doing yoga. But now I've started cramping.' Her eyes shimmered with tears as she looked up at him. 'I phoned Kate. She's phoning for an ambulance and then she's coming.'

Raphael's heart contracted. She had gone to someone else—not him—when she had needed help. She must really hate him. But he couldn't let himself think of that right now. All that mattered was making sure that Annie was all right. Even the baby…his heart twisted…wasn't as important as Annie.

In the distance he could hear the wail of the ambulance and the door opened and Kate burst in, carrying her medical bag.

'Dr Castillo. I didn't realise you were here. What's going on?'

'I haven't had time to make an assessment,' he said. 'But I'm afraid it sounds as if Annie has gone into labour.'

Hearing his words, Annie moaned again and folded in on herself. Raphael had never seen such anguish before. But she mustn't give up hope. Not yet.

He crouched down beside her and lifted her chin, forcing her to look into his eyes.

'Listen to me, Annie,' he said. 'I am going to do everything we can to save our baby. You have to believe that. Okay?' It took every bit of strength to keep his voice steady, but he couldn't let Annie see how terrified he was.

Annie looked back at him, her eyes wide with

pain and fear. But he saw resolve in her eyes. His Annie was stronger than she realised.

Kate passed him the Sonicaid from her bag so he could listen to the foetal heart. He felt almost weak with relief when he heard a steady beat.

'Baby's heartbeat is strong, Annie. We can do a better assessment when we get you to hospital.' He could hear the wail of the ambulance getting closer. 'Perhaps we'll be able to give you steroids. There may still be a chance we can stop labour.'

He looked over at Kate.

'Can you gather a couple of things, please? I will go with Annie in the ambulance.'

'I'm coming, too,' Kate said firmly. 'Annie is my patient as well as my friend. As far as this baby is concerned, you are the father and not in the best position to make clear-headed judgements. Rob is over at mine, so Jem will be fine.' She took Annie's hand. 'I'll stay with you as long as you need me.' Then she looked at Raphael. 'As long as you both need me.'

Raphael took one look at the determined set of the senior midwife's mouth. He was glad she would be around. Annie needed all the help she could get. She was all that mattered.

Annie was barely aware of being lifted into the ambulance. All she knew was that the pains were stronger and becoming more frequent. She searched Raphael's and Kate's eyes as they bent over her, looking for any sign of optimism, but their expressions were guarded. However she felt about Raphael, she was glad he was there with her. Between him and Kate, Annie knew her baby had the best possible chance, but, if they didn't manage to stop her labour, then her baby would be born at twenty-eight weeks. Annie knew only too well that even if it survived, the chances of complications were hugely increased.

Raphael must have read her mind. He gathered her in his arms, pulling her head against his chest. She felt safe, as if he could protect her from her worst fears.

'We will give you a tocolytic when we get you to hospital,' he said. 'We may still be in time to stop your labour. If we aren't, the baby still has a good chance. Many babies of that gestation do well. You need to remember that.'

'And many don't,' Annie mumbled into his chest. She couldn't even cry now, the fear was too intense. All she wanted was for her baby to live.

Then she was being lifted out of the ambulance. Raphael was shouting orders and Kate was holding her hand. There were lights and people and fear and pain. Then she was in one of the side rooms in the labour ward. Kate was examining her and Annie heard her tell everyone that she was five centimetres dilated. And there was another obstetrician and Julie. Where had she come from? And her obstetrician, Dr Gibson, was talking to Raphael. She couldn't hear what they were saying, but she heard the word *paediatrician* and *too late* and she was more frightened than ever. But Raphael was by her side again.

'It's too late to stop labour,' he said gently. She looked up and she could see the concern and sympathy in Julie and Kate's eyes.

'Look at me,' Raphael commanded. So she forced herself to look at him, not wanting to, knowing that whatever she saw there would be the truth and she wasn't ready for the truth—she'd never be ready.

Her eyes found his and she read the anguish there. He couldn't hide it from her, no matter how much he wanted to.

'You're going to have our baby—soon.' Annie looked away, but he eased her head around. 'Everyone is ready to help. The paediatrician is here and as soon as the baby is delivered he will be taken up to the special care nursery. They will do everything they can up there to keep our baby alive. Right now, you have to listen to Julie and Kate. And I'll be right here.'

'Don't leave me,' she whispered through lips frozen with fear.

'I'll never leave you, *cariño*. I'm staying right here. Where I belong.'

Two hours later Annie gave a final push and felt her child slip into the world and into Kate's waiting arms. Desperately she listened, waiting for a sound to let her know her baby lived. She watched as Julie rushed the baby over to the waiting incubator as she and the paediatrician started working over the tiny form.

'You have a little girl,' Kate said. 'Well done.'

'Can I see her?' Annie asked. More than

anything else she wanted to hold her baby in her arms. It could well be the last chance she had.

'We need to let Julie and the paediatrician do what they have to, Annie. Let them take care of our daughter,' Raphael said, but she could see his eyes were shining with unshed tears.

Tentatively she reached out her hand and brushed a lock of hair away from his eyes. 'Is she breathing? Please, Raphael, go to her.'

Raphael left her side, to be replaced by Kate.

'She is breathing, Annie,' she said. 'And although she's very small, she has a good chance. They'll be taking her away to Special Care as soon as they have her stabilised. They'll take you up to see her in a little while. Try and rest now. I promise you, one of us will let you know the second we have news.'

Annie looked past her to the incubator, but there were too many bodies in the way for her to see properly. She struggled to sit up. She needed to see her baby. Her daughter needed to feel her mother's presence. But Kate pressed her back down.

'Annie, we still need to deliver the placenta. And you'll only get in the way. I know it's horrible, but you need to let us do our job.'

Kate was right, of course. But it was so damned hard not being able to see her child. But just then a tiny cry filtered into the room. Her baby was crying. That was a good sign. There was a flurry of activity around the cot and Raphael came back to stand next to Annie.

'They are taking her upstairs just now,' he said. 'But she is breathing. She is beautiful. The most beautiful baby I have ever seen.' His voice cracked.

Hope flared as she saw the look of wonder in his eyes. He wouldn't look like that if her baby wasn't all right, would he? If she couldn't be with their daughter, at least Raphael could. Her baby wouldn't be alone.

'Go with them,' she whispered. 'Stay with her. She needs you.'

Suddenly the atmosphere in the room changed. 'She's haemorrhaging,' Dr Gibson called out. 'Get me some hemabate stat.' There was a flurry of activity and Annie felt panic clench her throat. Who was bleeding? What was happening?

Then Raphael's face swam into view. 'You have a bit of retained placenta,' he said quietly. 'They are giving you something to stop the bleeding.'

'We need to get her to theatre.' It was Dr Gibson. 'Julie, ring down and tell theatre to get ready for us. Then page the anaesthetist. C'mon, everyone, let's get moving.'

Raphael brushed a lock of hair from Annie's eyes. 'Don't be frightened, *cariño*. Everything's going to be okay. You'll be back on the ward before you know it.'

Annie clutched at his hand, amazed at her own strength. 'I need to see my baby before I go. Please. Just in case…' Her voice caught on a sob. She willed Raphael to understand. If anything went wrong, she might never see her baby.

'There isn't time,' he said. 'We can't afford to wait. We have to take you now.'

'Please, Raphael. Do this for me?'

She could see the hesitation in his eyes. But then he straightened.

'Let her see our baby,' he said urgently.

'There's no time,' Dr Gibson said. 'We have to operate on her *now*. She could bleed out.'

But Raphael moved towards the incubator. 'It will only take a second,' he said, and, picking up the tightly swaddled infant, he brought her over to Annie.

Annie gazed down at her child. She was barely the size of Raphael's hands and she could see every vein in her translucent skin. As she looked at her Annie knew that she would never again experience the powerful emotions that swept through her body. This was her child, and she would fight tooth and nail for her for the rest of her life.

There was a hush in the room as everyone stopped for a second to watch Annie meet her child.

'You fight,' Annie said to her daughter. 'Don't you dare leave me.'

'We need to take you down to theatre now,' Raphael said gently, and Annie knew that her brief moment with her baby was over. 'I'll be there with you.'

'No, Raphael,' Annie said, mustering the last of her strength. 'You go with our daughter. Please. I'll be all right.'

'I don't want to leave you on your own.' He looked after his departing child, obviously torn.

'She needs you more than I do. Besides, Kate is here. Come and tell me as soon as there is any news. Promise?'

He leaned over and brushed the top of her head with his lips. 'Everything is going to be all right. I'll be back as soon as I can.'

When Annie next opened her eyes, it was to find Raphael looking down at her. Fear clutched her chest but before she could speak, Raphael smiled.

'They stopped the bleeding. They had to put an intra-uterine balloon in but it will be removed shortly. You are going to be OK.'

Dazed, Annie looked around. She had a drip in her arm, but apart from feeling a little groggy she was fine. She licked dry lips and, without asking, Raphael poured a glass of water and, slipping his arm behind her shoulders, lifted her slightly so that she could drink. The water was enough to ease Annie's throat sufficiently to speak.

'Where is she? Is she all right? I want to see her.'

'Hey, take it easy, Annie. She's upstairs in Intensive Care. They have her on a respirator, but she's doing well. Our daughter is beautiful.'

Annie saw the wonder in his deep brown eyes. But she needed to see her child for herself. That was the only way she could believe that she was all right. She pushed the sheets aside just as

Julie entered the room. Annie had worked with Julie many times before and knew the experienced midwife well.

'And just what do you think you are doing?' Julie said, lifting Annie's legs and popping her back into bed.

'I want to see my child, Julie,' Annie said. 'Then I'll come back to bed. I promise.'

'No way,' Julie said firmly. It was a different side to the midwife, one that Annie hadn't seen before, but, then, she hadn't been a patient before. 'You are not leaving this bed. Not until I say so.'

Annie looked across at Raphael. She had to see their daughter. She just had to.

'Raphael, please. Tell them I can go upstairs. Only for a moment. I'll do as I'm told after that.'

Raphael looked at Annie. His eyes softened. 'I'll take responsibility,' he said. 'We'll take the drip with us and put her in a wheelchair. She's so stubborn, if we don't take her she'll be up there as soon as we aren't looking, anyway.'

Julie looked indecisive, but before she could protest further, Raphael was helping Annie out of bed.

'I don't need a wheelchair,' Annie protested,

but then as her legs buckled she had to lean on Raphael for support.

'It's a wheelchair or nothing,' Julie said. 'Just give me a mo' to fetch one.'

Annie didn't have the strength to argue. Besides, she didn't want to wait a moment longer to see her baby. Only when she saw her for herself would she truly believe what Raphael had told her.

But it was almost more than she could bear when she finally saw her tiny baby. She was almost hidden from view by wires, her face covered by the ventilator that was breathing for her, and Annie felt cold with dread. More than anything in the world she wanted to hold her daughter. Transfer the strength from her own body to that of her child. Let her know that she was there.

'Remember, it looks worse than it is,' Raphael said, resting his hands on her shoulders. 'The lines and wires are there to monitor her as much as anything.'

Annie nodded. She knew all that, of course she did. Plenty of her mothers over the years had had babies that required time in Special Care.

But it was one thing telling a mother not to be frightened by the paraphernalia of Special Care and quite another when it was your baby lying there. So small and so helpless.

She slipped a hand through the hole in the incubator and slipped a finger into her daughter's minuscule hand. Her heart filled with wonder as she felt the small fingers close around hers.

'Hello, darling,' she whispered. 'This is your mummy. Everything is going to be okay. But you have to fight.' Turning to Raphael, she could see his anguish in eyes. 'I want you to tell me everything the paediatrician has told you. I don't want to be protected, so keep nothing back from me.' She meant every word. Whatever terror gripped her, she was going to stay strong. Her baby needed her and until she was out of danger… She pushed the thought away. One step at a time.

'As you can see, she is being ventilated. Her lungs aren't fully developed yet, so she'll probably stay on it for a few days at least. They are also giving her surfactant to help her breathing.'

'What about…?' She could hardly bare to say the words, but Raphael guessed what she wanted to know.

'We won't know whether there are any complications—if she's suffered any—until later, Annie. She has to get through the next few days first.' He laid a hand on her shoulder and squeezed. 'Come on, let's get you back to bed. I'll come back up here and stay with her while you sleep.'

'I can't leave her,' Annie whispered.

'You are going to need all your strength in the next few days. And she is going to need her mother fit and healthy.'

'How can I sleep when she is fighting for her life?' But even as she said the words Annie felt a wave of fatigue wash over her. She was so tired.

'You can't stay here, Annie. The nurses need to work on her. But you can come back later, when you have had a rest. You lost a great deal of blood earlier.' He looked at his watch. 'It will be morning soon.'

Reluctantly Annie let Raphael take her back to her room and help her back into bed. 'You will wake me if there is any change, no matter how small?'

'Of course.'

'And you won't leave her?' She clutched his hand. 'I know you must be tired, too.'

'I won't leave her,' he promised. 'I'll watch over her while you sleep.'

Knowing he would be true to his word, Annie closed her eyes and gave in to sleep.

It was getting light when Annie next opened her eyes. As the memory of the night before came flooding back, she panicked.

Her baby. She needed to see her baby. Where was Raphael? Why wasn't he here to let her know what was happening? If he was still in Special Care, did that mean something had happened? Knowing that if she called for a nurse they would try and prevent her from getting out of bed, she pushed the bed covers aside and reached for the dressing gown Kate had packed for her. Then on legs that felt like rubber she slipped upstairs and into the special care nursery.

She found Raphael in a chair by the side of the incubator. He was leaning forward, gazing into the incubator and talking quietly in Spanish. Annie stood silently listening. Although she couldn't understand the words, she knew by the timbre of his voice that he was suffering too.

He must have felt her standing behind him because he turned. Annie drew a sharp breath when she saw his face. He looked gaunt with fatigue, his eyes were shadowed and there were lines on his face that Annie had never seen before. Clearly he hadn't left their baby's side, not even to change or shave. He had told her that he would watch over their baby and he had. There was no doubt he cared about his daughter, but would he feel the same way if she turned out to be less than perfect?

'There's no change. I was going to come and see you,' he said. 'The nurses were supposed to ring up as soon as you were awake.'

'They didn't know. I slipped out when no one was looking. I know the night sister well and she would have tried to stop me. I didn't want to take that risk.' She bent over the cot. Her daughter was still on the respirator and there were wires everywhere. But she was alive. That was all that mattered.

Raphael stood next to her.

'Have you thought of a name? We should name her.'

Annie felt fear claw her throat again. Why

was he so keen? Was he about to suggest that they had her baptized—just in case? She shook her head.

'I would like to call her Angela, after my mother.' She took a deep steadying breath and clenched her hands so hard that the nails dug into her palms.

Raphael put his arms around her and held her close. For a moment she resisted, then as he whispered her name she couldn't help herself. She clung to him as she gave in to her grief and fear.

'Angela. Little Angelica. It is a good name,' he murmured into her hair.

And then she was only vaguely aware of Raphael leading her away from the cot and into the staff room. The nurses, seeing her distress, quietly stood up and left them alone. Raphael sat in one of the easy chairs and, still holding her, pulled her onto his lap as if she were a child. She wound her arms around his neck and cried until eventually her tears subsided to hiccups.

She hid her face in his chest. She felt safe there, as if nothing bad could ever happen as long as this man held her. He slid a handkerchief

under her bowed head and she took it gratefully, using it to dry her face then blow her nose
noisily. Eventually she sneaked a glance at his
face, knowing, but not caring, that she must
look a mess.

'I'm sorry,' she said. 'I don't usually cry like
that, at least not in front of people.'

As he looked down at her with warm brown
eyes she suddenly realised she was still curled up
in his lap. Embarrassed, she struggled to her feet,
but he put a restraining arm around her waist.

'You must not apologise. Not everyone can be
strong all the time, and this is a terrible time for
you. But you are not alone. Not any longer. I am
here with you.'

He sounded more Spanish, almost as if
emotion had robbed him of his hitherto perfect
English. But he was suffering too. This was a
child he had also longed for. But what if Angela
didn't pull through? There was nothing to stop
Raphael walking away—and she wouldn't try to
stop him. Once again she realised how little she
actually knew about this man. She loved him,
there was no doubt about that, but if he chose to
walk away, she would let him.

She rested her head back on his chest and felt him rest his chin on top of her head. They sat there for a while longer, not saying anything, each one alone with their thoughts.

Eventually Annie eased herself out of his arms. 'I'm going to have a shower and get dressed so I can spend the rest of the day with Angela. Then you could go home and get some rest yourself. You must be exhausted.'

'I'm used to not sleeping.' He smiled up at her.

'No argument,' Annie said firmly. 'I want you back here later this afternoon awake and alert. Neither of us will be any use to Angela if we are falling asleep on our feet.'

Raphael looked surprised. He raised an eyebrow at her and a small smile tugged at the corner of his mouth.

'You must be feeling better, *cariño*, to be wanting to boss me about.'

Annie's heart melted at the look in his eyes. How she wished everything could be different. If only Raphael could love her, nothing would be impossible.

'Go,' he said, tipping her gently off his lap. 'There is something I need to tell you. But now is not the right time. Soon, I hope. When our child is safe, we will talk. But for now let us do what we have to.'

CHAPTER TWELVE

KATE finished packing the box of fruit, home-made jam and crusty rolls she had bought down at the farmers' market earlier that morning. Although she knew Annie wouldn't feel hungry, she hoped she'd be tempted by the snacks. Chloe was due to pick her up shortly so that the two women could go and see Annie together. They wouldn't stay long, just long enough to let Annie know that they were there if she needed them.

Poor Annie. The next few days, even weeks would be awful for her. But all they could do now was hope.

She thought about what she had found that morning when she'd been showering, and wondered what to do. See a doctor, obviously, although the lump was bound to be nothing. If only Rob wasn't away, she could have discussed it with him. Put it in perspective. She'd told herself a hundred times already that it was probably only a cyst, but the small voice in her head wouldn't go away. What if it wasn't? What then?

The slamming of a car door announced Chloe's arrival.

'Are you ready?' Chloe asked as she came into the kitchen. 'Yum, is that some of the Trevellyans' fab cheese?' she said, pinching a piece and popping it into her mouth. Then she looked at Kate sharply and frowned.

'There hasn't been bad news from the hospital, has there?' she asked anxiously.

'No, the baby's doing okay. If she had taken a turn for the worse, someone would have phoned us.'

'What is it, then? You're looking a bit tired.'

Kate laid her hands on the worktop. She didn't want to burden Chloe with her worries, but she hadn't counted on her friend's intuition.

Chloe came across and laid an arm across her shoulder. 'Kate, I can see something's wrong. You know you can talk to me about anything. Is it Rob? Are you two having problems? Or Jem?'

'No, Jem's fine. He's at football practice. And

Rob and I are getting on fine. More than fine, in fact. He's so good to me, and fun to be with. I'd forgotten what that was like.'

'Mmm. He is lovely. And Jem seems to get on with him—unless there are problems there? Or is it Nick? Has he said something to upset you?'

Kate realised that Chloe wasn't going to give up. She knew something was wrong and was clearly determined to get to the bottom of it. The young midwife was the closest thing she had to a best friend. One of the few people who knew the truth about Jem. And Nick.

'I felt a lump in my breast this morning when I was showering,' Kate finally admitted. 'I know it's probably nothing but…'

'But you're going to get it checked out,' Chloe finished for her. 'God, Kate, you must be scared stupid. So the sooner you see someone the better. Have you spoken to any of the doctors? What about Rob? Does he know?'

'Rob's away and it's Saturday so, no, I haven't seen anyone. I only discovered it this morning and I had to go to the farmers' market and I want to see Annie. I'll make an appointment to see Oliver next week.'

'Just like you, Kate, to put the needs of others before your own. You're always taking care of other people and forgetting about yourself. But for once I'm not going to let that happen,' Chloe said firmly. 'Oliver is doing the Saturday morning surgery. I'm positive he'll see you today.'

Chloe ignored Kate's protests about not wanting to bother anyone. She was right, of course, it wasn't an emergency and another day or two wasn't going to make any difference, but she dialled the number of the surgery anyway and asked to be put through to Oliver.

'Hello, darling. Yes, everything's fine. It's Kate. She needs to see someone. Straight away. I mean not in front of any life-and-death emergencies, but today, nevertheless.'

Kate couldn't hear the response on the other end of the line.

'She'll be there,' Chloe said firmly, before disconnecting the call and turning to Kate. 'He can see you at the end of surgery. About twelve? That way we can still go and see Annie if you want.'

Kate gave in, knowing it was useless to argue. 'I promised her I would. So if it's okay with you, I'd like to go as planned. But I had no idea you could be so bossy.' She smiled to show there was no malice in the words. 'You're always so mild-mannered with your patients.'

Chloe smiled back. 'I suspect it's the only way I'll get you to do as you're told.'

Suddenly Kate felt frightened.

'God, Chloe. What if it is cancer? What about Jem? I couldn't bear to leave my son alone. And Polly, the new GP. I persuaded her to come back to Penhally and said I'd be here to support her. She'll be here any day now. Now all this…'

Chloe hugged her fiercely. 'Slow down, Kate. Everything's going to be all right. Remember we have some of the best doctors in the world between here and St Piran's. And as you said, it could be nothing. Maybe just a cyst. Let's just wait and see what Oliver has to say.'

Kate knew that Chloe was right. There was no point in worrying until she had to. And right now she had a patient to see. Annie needed her support.

After checking on Angela, Annie returned to her room for a shower. She kept it short, anxious not to be away from the special care nursery too long.

When she emerged feeling almost human, it

was to find Chloe and Kate sitting on her freshly made bed, waiting for her. The sight of her two friends broke the control Annie had been so desperately clinging to. Kate opened her arms and Annie let her hold her as she gave in to the anguish and fear of the last few days. It seemed that Kate was always there whenever Annie needed someone. In the absence of her mother, who was desperately trying to get a flight back to the UK, Kate was the next best thing.

Annie wiped her eyes and managed a shaky laugh. 'For someone who hardly ever cries, that's all I seem to have been doing lately.'

'Hey,' Chloe said gently. 'We all need to let go sometimes. And these are exceptional circumstances. How is she, anyway?'

Annie brought them up to date. There wasn't really that much to tell. The next few days would be critical. 'If Angela survives…' Annie choked on the word but took a steadying breath before continuing, 'Then the next hurdle will be whether her brain has been damaged.'

Kate reached out a soothing hand. 'Everyone is rooting for you both,' she said softly. 'How is Raphael holding up?'

'He's been wonderful,' Annie admitted. 'He's hardly left her side. But he's agreed to go home for a bit as soon as I get back up.' She tried a smile. It was weak, but the best she could manage. 'I don't suppose anyone could bring me some clothes from home? I could ask Raphael, I suppose…'

'Tra-la.' Kate smiled, holding up a small case. 'We called by your house on our way in—I held onto your key last night. I think you'll find everything there. I don't think you can trust a man in these circumstances. He might remember the top, but forget the trousers!'

'You're a love,' said Annie gratefully, and, taking the bag from Kate, rummaged around. 'Bless you, you remembered everything—even my deodorant.'

Kate whipped out another carrier bag. 'I brought you something to eat as well. I popped down to the farmers' market this morning and selected some goodies to tempt you. It's my guess you haven't had anything for some time.'

Annie felt her throat close at the gesture. It was so typical of Kate and Chloe and she really appreciated her friends' support.

'I'm sorry, sweetheart, but I'm going to have to get back. I have a patient who is due to deliver very soon and I promised I'd go and see her,' Chloe said apologetically. 'But I'll pop in later if I get the chance.'

Chloe looked at Kate. 'Call me later?'

Kate nodded. Annie thought she looked tired. There were lines of tension around her mouth she hadn't noticed before.

'Thank you both so much for coming. I know you both have your own lives to be getting on with. And I want to get back upstairs, anyway,' Annie said.

'Hey,' Kate said. 'What are friends for? You know you can call me any time.' She kissed Annie on the cheek. 'Take care. I'll see you soon.'

Annie returned to the special care ward to be given the welcome news that Angela had been taken off the respirator. Instead, two tubes had been inserted into Angela's nostrils and she could see her baby's face clearly for the first time. Her breath caught as she gazed down on the beloved features of her child. Angela's lips were like seashells washed in the ocean, her miniature nose perfect. She has Raphael's hair, Annie thought, taking in the dark hair that covered her head. Carefully she inserted a hand into the incubator and stroked the downy skin of her baby.

She knew then that she would stand between her child and a tank or a tidal wave or a stalking tiger. She would lay down her life without a moment's hesitation over and over again if she had to, but right now she could do nothing for her child. Nothing except wait and watch over her. She became aware of a presence behind her and she didn't have to turn to know it was Raphael.

'If I lose her…' Her voice cracked and she had to take a deep breath before she could continue. 'If I lose her, I don't know what I'll do. I can't imagine wanting to go on.'

She felt his hand on her shoulder and then he turned her so that she was facing him. Placing a finger under her chin, he tilted her head, forcing her to meet his gaze.

'Don't say that. Never say that. You are stronger than you think. And anyway, I told you I will not let anything happen to her.' His voice was low and urgent, his need to convince her evident in every syllable. Annie desperately wanted to believe him. She dropped her eyes to his achingly tender mouth before slowly raising her eyes to his. Through her fear she could see her pain reflected in his eyes. He too needed comfort, but Annie couldn't offer him any.

'*Cariño,*' he said, his voice a river of anguish. '*Te quiero con toda mi alma.* I love you with all my soul. You and our daughter are my heart, my soul, my future. All I ever want and all I will ever need.' Annie's heart thumped lurched.

Had he really said he loved her? Could he mean it?

He took her hand and placed it on his chest. She could feel the pounding of his heart through the thin fabric.

'Do you feel that?' he demanded.

Despite her grief, Annie felt a small smile tug at the corner of her mouth. It was such a Latin gesture. She nodded, the emotion welling up inside her preventing her from speaking.

'As long as my heart keeps beating, I will not let anything happen to you or our child.'

But however much she wanted to believe him, she couldn't. It wasn't in his power to promise anything. Least of all that their child would live.

* * *

Kate slipped off the examination couch and picked up her blouse, sliding her arms into the sleeves. Oliver waited until she had finished and was settled in the chair opposite him before he spoke.

'There is a lump there. I can feel it the upper left quadrant. As you said, it could be nothing, a cyst perhaps, but I think we should get it checked out all the same.'

Kate could read the concern in his brown eyes. He was being matter-of-fact, but she could read him like a book. He didn't believe it was a cyst and neither did she.

'Does Rob know?' Oliver continued. 'Can he go with you to the hospital? It's Saturday but I might be able to get one of the surgeons to come in and see you. They'll probably want to do a fine needle biopsy and a mammogram.'

'Rob's away this weekend. He's gone up north to see his mother. I would have gone with him if it hadn't been for Jem.' She stood up and went to look out the window. The day, which had started off dull and threatening to rain, had turned into one of those perfect days. In the distance she could see the tips of the waves as they rolled to shore. There were quite a few boats out as well, a mixture of fishing trawlers and yachts. Kate wished she were out there with them, far away from talk of lumps and biopsies and far away from the terror of what it would mean for her son if she turned out to have cancer. She thought about Annie. Her hopes and fears tied up with the tiny life she had given birth to, and all the other people, not just in Penhally Bay but all over the world who would be facing the same uncertainties and fears as she was.

'I can wait my turn like everyone else,' Kate said. 'A day or two isn't going to make much difference.'

'Are you sure you don't want me to phone Ben? He'll know who you should see.'

'No,' Kate said heavily. 'I don't want to jump the queue. It's not fair to every other frightened woman out there. Besides, by the time my appointment comes through, Rob will be back.'

'There's only a week waiting time for urgent appointments,' Oliver said. 'And I'm going to grade yours as urgent.'

Kate smiled wanly. 'Okay,' she said. Just then

there was a knock on the door and Nick stuck his head around it.

'Oh, Oliver. I'm sorry. I thought you had finished seeing patients.' Then he noticed Kate and he looked surprised. 'Kate! I didn't think you were in today. Is there something up with one of your patients?' His eyes narrowed. Something in her and Oliver's expression seemed to alert him that Kate's presence was unusual.

'I just had something I wanted to talk over with Oliver,' she said hastily. Well, it was true. But let think Nick it was about a patient.

'There's nothing wrong, is there?' he asked. He walked over to the desk and crouched down next to Kate. 'You would tell me if there was something wrong, wouldn't you?' Kate felt her heart tighten at the obvious concern in his eyes. Whatever problems they might have had, were *still* having, she knew that somewhere deep down inside Nick cared about her, even if it was as just a friend. But that didn't mean she was ready to share her worries with him. He had made it clear often enough that he wasn't prepared to offer her more than the professional support of a colleague. And one thing Kate couldn't bear was for him to feel sorry for her.

She laughed, but the sound was hollow even to her own ears.

'What possibly could be wrong, Nick, that I couldn't cope with on my own?' She didn't mean the words to have such a bitter quality to them, but she couldn't help herself. The one thing she truly wanted from Nick, acceptance of the child they shared, he wasn't able to give her.

'If you're sure?' Nick said, straightening. He sounded less than convinced but Kate knew him well enough to know that he wouldn't probe. One thing you could say about him was that he respected her privacy. He turned back to Oliver, who was watching the exchange quietly. Kate wondered if he had picked up on the tension that seemed to be a permanent feature between her and Nick these days. 'I wondered if you fancied a round of golf this afternoon?' he asked. 'Dragan and Ben are up for it if you are.'

'Sure,' Oliver said. 'I think Chloe has plans for this afternoon, so I'm free.'

'How is Annie?' Nick asked. 'Has anyone spoken to her?'

'I saw her this morning,' Kate said. 'She's okay. Raphael is with her.'

'Raphael? Dr Castillo?' Nick said, looking puzzled.

Oliver and Kate exchanged a smile. Good grief, Kate thought, Nick could be so dense sometimes, completely failing to see what was right underneath his nose.

CHAPTER THIRTEEN

A WEEK after their baby had been born Annie and Raphael sat in the easy chairs the staff had provided and watched over their child. The lights had been turned low, although the nurses and doctors still tended their tiny charges with the same dedication and attentiveness that they did during the day.

Annie rested her eyes, thinking back to what Raphael had said. He had called her his heart and his soul. But surely these were just the words of a man in emotional turmoil to the woman who was locked there with him? She still couldn't believe that he meant them.

'Maybe she'll be a piano player,' he said suddenly into the silence. 'She has your long fingers.' He picked up Annie's hand in one of his. 'Such beautiful hands.' Annie looked down at her hands in surprise. She had never thought of her hands as being beautiful before, but perhaps he was right. Her fingers were long and shapely.

'Why did you come back?' she asked. 'You know, the night Angela was born after we…' She tailed off, blushing furiously, but she wanted to know. Everything had happened so fast it was only now that she had begun to wonder.

He turned towards her, his eyes glowing in the semi-darkness. 'I came back because…because I realised something important. When this is over, I'm going to do everything to win you properly. Make you believe me when I tell you that I want to marry you. Because I love you.'

Annie started to say something but he stopped her words with his fingertip.

'I want us to start over. Do everything as it should have been. How it was meant to be.'

Annie felt something deep down inside her blossom at his words. Could she dare to believe that he meant what he was saying? And did he truly understand what he was saying?

'Don't. Please, Raphael. Don't say any more.' She flinched at the naked pain in his eyes, but forced herself to go on.

'I can't have any more children. You must know that. Angela was miraculous enough. If we marry, you will be signing yourself up to a lifetime of childlessness.' Her voice broke on the words. 'If…' she faltered, but forced herself to go on. 'God forbid, but if Angela doesn't pull through, there will be no more children.'

'I would be signing myself up for a lifetime with the woman I love,' Raphael said firmly. 'The woman without whom life has no meaning—a dark and empty place. Don't you know that when I am with you my life is full of light? I told you before and I will tell you again and keep on telling you until you believe me— you are all I need.'

'You would give up everything for me?' Annie whispered, hardly daring to believe he meant what he was saying.

'I would give my life for you if I had to.' He crouched by her side. 'I have been so foolish. Can you ever forgive me? How could I have ever believed even for the smallest second—' he held out two fingers millimetres apart '—that you were anything except the strong, loving, honest woman you are?'

'Because you believed it once before and she betrayed you,' Annie said, unable to bear the self-reproach in his eyes. 'I can understand.'

'I know I don't deserve you. I am full of mistakes…' Annie hid a smile. His English only ever suffered when his feelings ran high. 'But if you marry me, I will spend the rest of my life proving I am worthy of you. If you want to adopt a little brother or sister for our sweet daughter, I would be happy too.'

Annie still wasn't sure. He might mean it now, but later, in years to come, he might come to regret having married her, and that was one thing she would never allow. She would rather let him go—even if it broke her heart—than see him become resentful of her. But before she could formulate the words there was the sound of an alarm going off at Angela's cot. Within seconds the incubator was surrounded. Annie looked at Raphael, terrified.

Quickly the paediatrician attached Angela to a machine again and after a few agonising minutes the monitor stopped bleeping as Angela's breathing returned to normal.

After listening to Angela's chest, the paediatrician turned to Annie and Raphael.

'I think your daughter has patent ductus arteriosus, or PDA as we call it. As you both are probably aware, the blood circulating in the foetus doesn't go through the lungs but bypasses the lungs via an artery. Normally this artery closes itself soon after birth, but in pre-term babies such as yours, it sometimes fails to close.'

Raphael nodded. 'I've seen it before.'

'We've been giving her drugs for a day or two to try and close it that way, but that doesn't seem to have worked…'

'So you'll need to do it surgically,' Raphael finished for him.

'But she's so small,' Annie interjected.

Raphael turned to Annie and took both of her hands in his. He looked at her steadily, his brown eyes calm.

'It's her best chance,' he said. 'The surgeons are used to operating on babies of Angela's size. We have to trust them to do what's best for her.'

Annie looked at her daughter. Lying in her cot, all alone attached to tubes and wires. Her child was totally dependent on her parents making the right decision. Annie felt so help-less. What if they made the wrong one? 'But what if…?' Annie couldn't bring herself to finish the sentence.

'Look at me, Annie,' Raphael demanded. Annie dragged her eyes away from her baby. Raphael's eyes burned with his need to convince her. 'Only you have the right to make the decision. I can't. But I love her, too. You have to trust me about this. Please.'

There was no doubting his pain. There was no doubting his love for their daughter. And she did trust him. They were together in this and would always be. Annie realised that never again would she be alone. She would always have Raphael to share impossible decisions with.

'Okay,' she whispered, 'I'll sign the consents.'

Annie and Raphael passed what seemed like hours while their daughter was in surgery, in almost complete silence. Annie laid her head on Raphael's lap and he gently stroked her hair. They waited in the relatives' room just along the corridor from theatre. Every now and again Raphael would ask Annie if he could get her anything. Water? Coffee? But she always shook her head. She knew she couldn't possibly swallow anything until she knew Angela was out of surgery. Eventually they heard footsteps coming down the corridor. Annie sat up, her heart in her throat, knowing that the moment of truth had arrived.

Raphael got to his feet and pulled Annie up and into his embrace. 'Whatever it is, be strong, my love. I am with you.'

The surgeon stepped into the family waiting room, a broad grin lighting up his face. It was the news they had both been desperately longing for. The paediatric surgeon explained that Angela had come through the surgery well and he expected her to make a full recovery. She was currently in Intensive Care but they could see her if they wanted. If they wanted!

Dr Nick Tremayne sat deep in thought. Something was up with Kate. He couldn't quite put his finger on it, but something was worrying her, he would bet his life on it. He crossed over to his consulting-room window and looked out. The perfect weather had turned again. The rain was falling in thick slabs, perfectly matching his gloomy mood. He didn't know why, but seeing Kate with her new partner made him feel uncomfortable. Not that it was any of his business. He should be glad she had found someone who could offer her a life free of complications. But, damn it, he hated seeing the way Jem responded to Rob. The way the growing boy seemed to look up to him, almost as if he had accepted that Rob was the father he had never known. And why should that bother him? Shouldn't he be glad that his son had a good man as a role model in his life? Rob was a decent man. Nick knew that. And it wasn't as if he could offer the child anything, no matter how much Kate had tried to convince him. Perhaps if he'd known that Jem was his son much much earlier. Perhaps then he could have found a way to be a father to him. But it was too late now. Every time he looked at the child he remembered that he had been unfaithful to his beloved wife, Annabel. What kind of man was he?

He sighed with exasperation. How had he managed to make such a mess of it all? He couldn't see a way to make things right.

A soft tap on the door and then Kate popped her head around. She was still beautiful, he thought. The years had been kind to her. Why couldn't he let her go and make a proper life for herself? Why did the thought of her being with someone else drive him crazy? It wasn't as if he had anything to offer her.

'Just to let you know that Chloe is doing the antenatal clinic on her own this afternoon and I'm taking the afternoon off. So she might need some help from you.'

Nick was surprised. It was unlike Kate to take time off, especially when she knew it would leave her colleagues short-handed.

'Is everything all right, Kate? There's nothing up with Jem, is there?'

'No, Jem's fine. He's at school. It's just I have something I need to do this afternoon.'

'Can't it wait?'

He could see the exasperation in Kate's eyes.

'It's not as if I ever ask for time off, Nick,' she said frostily.

Of course, she was right. If anything, she had put the patients' needs before her own for years. He knew that. It was just that he sensed she was keeping something from him. And he wanted to know what it was. But one look at the determined set of her mouth told him it would be useless to pry. He had given up all rights to Kate's personal life and they both knew it.

'Of course,' he said. 'Forgive me.' He thought he saw a flicker of disappointment in her eyes, but just as quickly it was gone. It seemed that he was forever destined to disappoint this woman.

'I'll see you tomorrow, then,' she said before closing the door behind her.

Kate perched on her chair, trying not to show how nervous she was. In the seat next to her, Rob looked as ill at ease as Kate felt. He had insisted on coming with her to St Piran's. At first Kate had tried to dissuade him, she was so used to doing everything on her own, but then relented. Rob cared about her. Why face something so difficult on her own when he so clearly wanted to be there to support her? He had waited outside while Dr Bower had performed a fine needle biopsy and then waited some more while Kate had a mammogram. The hour they had waited to be called into see the surgeon for the results was the one of the longest in Kate's life.

The surgeon, Dr Bower, an older woman Kate had met before through work, seemed to take her time looking through Kate's notes before removing her glasses and placing them carefully on the table. Kate was dimly aware of Rob reaching across and taking her hand. He gave it a reassuring squeeze and she was thankful she had let him come with her.

'I'm sorry, Kate,' Dr Bower was saying, 'but the tests have come back positive. The lump is cancerous. The good news is that the mammogram suggests that we have caught it at a very early stage. I'm fairly confident that we can get away with removing the lump without having to resort to a mastectomy, but I won't be sure until we have you on the table. If there is any sign that the cancer has invaded the lymph nodes then we might be facing a different scenario. In that case, a mastectomy may still be an option, followed by chemotherapy and radiotherapy. As I said, I don't think that's what we are facing here, but I think it's best that you know the worst possible outcome. One way or another, I suggest we get you in for the procedure as soon as possible.'

Kate felt her world tip and slide. Of course she had known that it could be cancer, but she hadn't allowed herself to believe it. The pressure of Rob's hand on hers grew stronger but she was barely aware of it. She had cancer. She could die. Her son could be left motherless, and—a sick feeling washed over her—fatherless. How could life be so unfair?

'Are you sure?' she managed through a mouth that felt as if it was stuffed with pebbles, it was so dry. 'I mean—I'm sorry, of course you're sure. We wouldn't be having this conversation if you weren't.'

'I know it's a shock,' Dr Bower said sympathetically. 'But as I said before, it's good news that we caught it so early. You'll want some time to take it all in, but I really want to schedule you in for theatre, possibly the week after next.' She consulted her diary. 'I have a slot in my diary for a week on Monday. Would that suit you?'

Kate could only manage a nod. Her mouth was still too dry to speak. What was she going to tell Jem?

Kate managed to hold it together until she and Rob were back in his car. But when Rob silently put his arms around her and held her close, the tears came. Rob let her cry while he stroked her hair and murmured soothing words of comfort. He waited until her sobs subsided.

Kate removed herself from his arms, miserably aware of her tear-stained cheeks and swollen eyes. She blew furiously on the handkerchief Rob held out for her.

'I'm sorry, Rob, to land you in all this. I don't think it's what you expected when you took up with me.'

'I took up with you, as you put it—' Rob smiled '—because you are the most wonderful woman I have ever met. I would rather be with you than anywhere else in the world. But I want you to listen to me.' He swivelled around in his seat and took Kate's hands in his. She felt the warmth of his touch ease away some of the chill that had been seeping through her body since Dr Bower had given her the diagnosis.

'Dr Bower said that they caught it very early and survival rates from breast cancer have improved enormously over the last few years. That is what you need to remember.'

Kate looked at his dear, kind face. He always made her feel so protected and loved. Why couldn't she feel about him the way he so obviously felt about her?

'I know,' she said. 'But all I can think about is Jem. There is a chance when they do the biopsy at the time of surgery that they'll find it's more advanced. What will happen to him if…?' She took an uneven breath. 'If the worse comes to the worst? I have to think about that. I'm all he has…I can't imagine what it would do to him to be left alone. He's still so young.' Her voice broke and she couldn't help the tears from falling once more.

Rob pulled her back into his arms. 'It's all right. You'll see. Everything will work out fine.'

But Kate knew it wasn't all right. Bad things happened. And even Rob couldn't promise her that everything would be all right. No matter how much she wanted to believe him.

In the following days, as their daughter got gradually stronger, Annie let herself think about what Raphael had said. In the days after Angela's surgery they hadn't spoken much. When Raphael wasn't with them he was back at work, putting in a full day before returning to the ward to sit with them both.

Annie wondered if, now that their child was out of danger, he regretted his words the night of Angela's surgery. But she wouldn't be the one to speak of it. If he had changed his mind, or in the cold light of day realised he didn't love her, she would accept that. In time the pain would ease and whatever happened she would always have her beloved daughter. It would be a few weeks yet before they would be able to take Angela home, but the nursery, with its sunshine-yellow walls and crib stuffed with soft toys, was ready and waiting for her.

Kate had been to see Annie often, as had the other members of Penhally Bay Surgery, and Annie had been overwhelmed by their love and support.

She leaned back in her chair as her child suckled. It had been a great joy to find that it was still possible and Annie revelled in the feel of her baby's skin close against hers.

Annie looked up to find Raphael standing looking down, his face filled with wonder. Her heart started racing. She knew without a shadow of doubt that she would never love anyone the way she loved him. When she had met him she had felt as if she had found the other half of her soul. And she still felt that way. She couldn't imagine a life without him. Not seeing him. Perhaps one day hearing that he had met someone else? But she also knew that she loved him too much to wish anything for him except happiness. Even if that life didn't include her. She loved him so much that she knew she could let him go. Even if it broke her heart.

'You look beautiful,' he said. 'How can I ever thank you for giving me the most precious gift in the world?'

He knelt by her side and touched her face with a gentle finger, before dropping his head and kissing the top of their child's head.

Annie felt her throat tighten. She wanted to imprint everything about him into her heart. Every facial feature, every expression, so in the months or years to come she would have her memories even if she didn't have him.

She replaced Angela in the incubator. She was only allowed to hold her for short periods, but she savoured every opportunity.

Raphael remained kneeling and reached a hand up and pulled her back down into the chair. Annie was uncomfortably aware of curious heads turning in their direction as the nurses stopped what they were doing to watch.

'I have something I want to ask you,' he said hoarsely. 'I was going to wait until we brought our baby home for good. But I can't sleep for not knowing what your answer would be.'

Annie studied him. He looked exhausted. The last few days of working while spending every moment with their child had taken their toll. There were dark shadows under his eyes and lines around his eyes that Annie hadn't seen before.

'I must know,' he said his voice tense. 'Do you think you could ever love me?'

Annie looked at him in wonder. Didn't he know? Hadn't he guessed how she felt? Without waiting for a reply, Raphael continued. 'From the moment I met you, I knew you were different. But I tried to tell myself it was impossible to fall in love with a woman I had only known so briefly. I couldn't let myself believe it. I wanted to contact you. I thought about it often, but I didn't. I thought it was better to keep my image of you alive and not risk having it smashed. And I still hoped there was a chance that I would win the court case for access to Sebastian on appeal. So I didn't listen to my heart. I let you go.'

Annie opened her mouth to speak, but he stopped her words with his finger. 'Please. I have to say this. Whatever happens, I have to tell you.'

Annie waited for him to continue, acutely aware of the tiny shivers of delight and hope darting through her.

'Then when you told me you were pregnant, I thought that it was fate, but I couldn't let myself hope. I needed to know that it was my child and if it was, I needed to know that I couldn't lose her. The thought of losing another child drove me crazy. But when I saw you again, as I got to know you, I realised that I hadn't made a mistake about you. You were everything I ever thought you were. Everything I had ever hoped to find in a woman. Kind, caring, beautiful and loyal.' He looked a bit sheepish for a moment as he realised that the staff as well as most of the patients were riveted to every word he was saying. Annie felt a smile spread over her face.

'I love you. I love you more than I thought it was possible to love a woman. I want to marry you. I want to spend the rest of my life making you happy, making you smile. I want us, you me and Angela, to be a family. It doesn't matter where. Here or Spain. All that matters is that I am with you.'

'Can I speak now?' Annie asked when he came to a halt. Her heart was singing. She couldn't wait to put him out of his misery.

'I love you too, Raphael Castillo. I have loved you since the moment I saw you. And there is nothing that would make me happier than to marry you.' She could see the triumph in his eyes as he took in her words. She let him pull her to her feet, dimly aware of the sound of clapping and cheering. But as she tilted her face to his she knew that finally she had everything she had ever dreamed of.

EPILOGUE

ANNIE walked down the aisle her hand on her father's arm. The church where she had first met Raphael had seemed to them both to be the logical place for their wedding. She passed Raphael's mother, who was holding Angela in her arms. Little Maria was pressed close to the older woman's side. From the moment she and Raphael had returned to Spain with their daughter, Maria had become Angela's self-appointed guardian. She and Raphael had decided to look into the possibility of adopting Maria. Although it was early days yet, the young girl's father had raised no objections and it looked as if in time they would have two daughters. And maybe in a couple of years they would investigate the possibility of adopting another child. But all that was in the future, Annie thought as Raphael turned to watch her approach. His eyes darkened as he looked at her and Annie blushed, knowing that he was thinking of their wedding night.

Since he had proposed they had taken it slowly, getting to know the little things about each other and falling deeper in love every day. They hadn't made love, even though it had almost driven them both crazy. They had agreed to wait until they were married and Annie felt a heat low in her abdomen as she thought about the night to come. They had also agreed that they would live in Spain for the time being. It made sense. Annie had no plans to go back to work until Angela was a little older and the last thing little Maria needed was more disruption. They would go back to the UK often on holiday to see her parents and friends and, of course, they would come to Spain to see them too. She heard a little cry as Angela stirred from her nap. Annie caught Raphael's eye as she stood beside him and prepared to make the vows that would bind them together for the rest of their lives. In his eyes she found just what she was looking for. Right now she had everything she had ever wanted. Right here in this church.

MEDICAL™

Large Print

Titles for the next six months…

June

SNOWBOUND: MIRACLE MARRIAGE	Sarah Morgan
CHRISTMAS EVE: DOORSTEP DELIVERY	Sarah Morgan
HOT-SHOT DOC, CHRISTMAS BRIDE	Joanna Neil
CHRISTMAS AT RIVERCUT MANOR	Gill Sanderson
FALLING FOR THE PLAYBOY MILLIONAIRE	Kate Hardy
THE SURGEON'S NEW-YEAR WEDDING WISH	Laura Iding

July

POSH DOC, SOCIETY WEDDING	Joanna Neil
THE DOCTOR'S REBEL KNIGHT	Melanie Milburne
A MOTHER FOR THE ITALIAN'S TWINS	Margaret McDonagh
THEIR BABY SURPRISE	Jennifer Taylor
NEW BOSS, NEW-YEAR BRIDE	Lucy Clark
GREEK DOCTOR CLAIMS HIS BRIDE	Margaret Barker

August

EMERGENCY: PARENTS NEEDED	Jessica Matthews
A BABY TO CARE FOR	Lucy Clark
PLAYBOY SURGEON, TOP-NOTCH DAD	Janice Lynn
ONE SUMMER IN SANTA FE	Molly Evans
ONE TINY MIRACLE…	Carol Marinelli
MIDWIFE IN A MILLION	Fiona McArthur

MILLS & BOON®

MEDICAL™

Large Print

September

THE DOCTOR'S LOST-AND-FOUND BRIDE	Kate Hardy
MIRACLE: MARRIAGE REUNITED	Anne Fraser
A MOTHER FOR MATILDA	Amy Andrews
THE BOSS AND NURSE ALBRIGHT	Lynne Marshall
NEW SURGEON AT ASHVALE A&E	Joanna Neil
DESERT KING, DOCTOR DADDY	Meredith Webber

October

THE NURSE'S BROODING BOSS	Laura Iding
EMERGENCY DOCTOR AND CINDERELLA	Melanie Milburne
CITY SURGEON, SMALL TOWN MIRACLE	Marion Lennox
BACHELOR DAD, GIRL NEXT DOOR	Sharon Archer
A BABY FOR THE FLYING DOCTOR	Lucy Clark
NURSE, NANNY…BRIDE!	Alison Roberts

November

THE SURGEON'S MIRACLE	Caroline Anderson
DR DI ANGELO'S BABY BOMBSHELL	Janice Lynn
NEWBORN NEEDS A DAD	Dianne Drake
HIS MOTHERLESS LITTLE TWINS	Dianne Drake
WEDDING BELLS FOR THE VILLAGE NURSE	Abigail Gordon
HER LONG-LOST HUSBAND	Josie Metcalfe

MILLS & BOON®

millsandboon.co.uk Community

Join Us!

The Community is the perfect place to meet and chat to kindred spirits who love books and reading as much as you do, but it's also the place to:

- Get the inside scoop from authors about their latest books
- Learn how to write a romance book with advice from our editors
- Help us to continue publishing the best in women's fiction
- Share your thoughts on the books we publish
- Befriend other users

Forums: Interact with each other as well as authors, editors and a whole host of other users worldwide.

Blogs: Every registered community member has their own blog to tell the world what they're up to and what's on their mind.

Book Challenge: We're aiming to read 5,000 books and have joined forces with The Reading Agency in our inaugural Book Challenge.

Profile Page: Showcase yourself and keep a record of your recent community activity.

Social Networking: We've added buttons at the end of every post to share via digg, Facebook, Google, Yahoo, technorati and de.licio.us.

www.millsandboon.co.uk